THE NARROW THREE

—⊶⊷—

J. K. MILLER II

First Piece Writing · Clearwater, Florida

For my mother, who continues to be my rock.
To my father, who always pushes me to grow.
To my family who have always been by my side.
To friends who have been so loyal, patient, and supportive.
To you, the readers, who keep my muse going.

From the bottom of my heart, thank you.

PROLOGUE

"Do you know why you're here, Nathan?"

The heat made it stuffy in the room and they had given him no water. The light above flickered every now and again, almost as if someone was controlling it from outside. White walls, the kind of white that wore on the eyes, surrounded them with only a small window watching them on the other side of the room. The neutral carpet, worn from heavy foot traffic, might as well have been hard wood. Everything about the room was set up to intimidate and piss off suspects. Even the air he breathed seemed to be different from normal air.

"Obviously," he said.

"Would you mind speaking it aloud? Just for the record's sake."

"You think I killed Emily Henderson."

"We believe you are a suspect, yes."

"On what grounds?"

The detective opened a manila folder he had brought with him and flopped it down atop the long, stainless steel table. He leaned forward, placing his elbows on the table and clasping his fingers together, extending his thumbs to his mouth. He stared with eyes hard from experience.

"Emily Henderson was found dead in her town home," he explained. "Her body had multiple cuts from a knife. Long cuts."

He pulled out four enlarged photos of the body. Long, deep lacerations were all along Ms. Henderson's naked front, some going from her waist up to her neck. It was a ghastly sight that turned Nathan's stomach.

"It seems the killer was very pissed off." The detective placed the last photo of her cut up face in front of him. "We found your DNA at the scene, Nathan."

"She was my girlfriend," Nathan replied without looking at the man. "I was over there all the time. You know how it is, David."

"Detective Johnson. We found *blood*, Nathan."

Nathan pulled out his lip to expose the stitches. "We got into an argument. She punched me."

"What was the fight about?"

"Argument," Nathan corrected. "She's the jealous type. Sees me talking to another woman and goes off the wall."

"And she punched you?"

"Yep."

"That must have pissed you off."

Nathan nodded admittedly. "I told her we were through and I left."

"Just like that?"

"Just like that."

Detective Johnson stared at Nathan over his knuckles. "So you're telling me that you and Emily got into a fight over you speaking to another woman, she punched you hard enough to knock the blood from your mouth, and you just *walk away?*"

Nathan shrugged. "I guess you'd have had to be there."

The detective was staring again; a piercing, steady gaze. It was as if he could see the crime on Nathan's forehead and was waiting for it all to play out. Nathan readjusted in the hard chair.

The detective's dark gray button up shirt that went well with the bold tie ruffled as he eased back in his chair. His dark hair was neatly combed back and the light glinted off his sharp features.

"I know you know something, Nathan."

"What do you want from me, Detective? I've told you everything I know."

"No you haven't."

"How would you know?"

"When you do this for as long as I have, you get to know when people are holding something back." He leaned forward slightly. "You're holding back, Nathan."

Nathan peered at the detective. "From the police or from *you?*"

That caught Johnson's attention. His face went blank as he stiffened.

"What's that supposed to mean?" he defiantly asked.

Nathan narrowed his eyes. "It means I know. I know you don't think I killed Emily. You don't even care about who this is. I know this "interrogation" is not being recorded. You're more interested in something else."

"Such as?"

"Such as why the blood did not match. And since the blood didn't match, that means that whoever this is," Nathan tapped one of the photos on the desk, "isn't who you're looking for."

Detective Johnson remained silent.

"So let's cut the bullshit," Nathan continued. "We both know this isn't Emily. Who is this?"

The stare returned, interested, impressed. Detective Johnson placed his clasped hands back on the table.

"She was targeted. Someone who was after the *real* Emily Henderson." He nodded slightly toward the photos. "This woman was paid three thousand dollars to take on Emily's identity."

"So she could get away," Nathan thought aloud.

"There is no trace of her ever being in this city. Everything comes back to this woman."

"So...why am I here, Detective?"

"We believe you know where Emily is."

"You mean *you* believe I know where Emily is."

"Are you saying you do?"

"I'm just saying." Nathan glanced around the room in thought. "What's in it for me?"

Detective Johnson's brows lifted as if he found Nathan's question amusing. "You don't get charged with this woman's murder."

"I told you I didn't kill her."

"Withholding information, impeding a criminal investigation. I believe that falls under Obstruction of Justice. You should know that. If you're lying about knowing where she is, how do I know you aren't lying about killing her?"

"You'll need more than that."

"This woman is dead and your DNA is at the scene. It's all the proof I need. Everything else will be up to the jury." The detective leaned forward again, his confidence returning. "Unless there's something you can tell me?"

Nathan lowered his eyes back down to the photographs. He shook his head slowly, looking off.

"I don't know where she is."

"Bullshit."

The detective said it calmly as if he knew Nathan was going to lie. Somehow it was more intimidating than if he had screamed it.

"If you really want to go to jail for this, that's fine with me," Detective Johnson said, rising from the chair. "It's a real shame for a man with your reputation."

"Alright," Nathan resigned with a sigh. "Alright."

The detective sat back down, clasping his hands together again. Nathan sighed a second time.

"I don't know where she is now, but I know she's going to Santa Fe."

"New Mexico?"

Nathan nodded. "Her flight leaves tomorrow morning."

"Did she tell you anything else?"

Nathan shook his head at first, then lifted his brows. "Actually, yes. 'He'll show himself.'"

"What?"

"That's all she said: 'He'll show himself'."

"By 'he', she means the killer?"

"You know Emily, she doesn't explain anything."

"Maybe you don't know her as well as you think you do."

The detective rose once again to leave the room.

"Maybe not," Nathan said, "but she knows your wife better than you do."

Detective Johnson froze halfway to the door.

"What are you talking about?" Johnson said.

"I think you know," Nathan replied. "How long had it been going on? Two months?"

The detective was silent.

"That must have been embarrassing for you," Nathan continued. "Looking in her eyes and seeing the emptiness you couldn't fill. We all have our limits and desires. I guess she just doesn't like men."

Johnson whirled and lunged at him. Nathan did nothing to resist as Johnson seized him by his shirt and easily lifted him out of the chair. It clattered to the floor as he was forced up against the wall.

"Where is she!" he demanded.

"I told you, Santa Fe tomorrow," Nathan said.

He was just able to brace himself as the detective's fist came around. The impact blurred his vision.

"I'll fucking kill you right here if you don't tell me!"

Nathan's eyes flashed down to the table. "Like you killed Nancy?"

"And I'll do it again!"

"Alright, alright, alright!"

Rage flared in the detective's eyes as he waited for an answer. Nathan could see the muscles in his jaw line bulging in his frustration.

"She's at the Holiday off Trexel," Nathan said.

"The one on the corner."

"Yeah. Room 425."

Detective Johnson shoved Nathan to the side. Nathan was just able to catch himself before he fell to the ground.

"There is one other thing you should know," Nathan said as Johnson was reaching for the handle. Nathan pulled his sidearm from the concealed holster in his waistband. "You're under arrest for the murder of Nancy Cummings."

"You have nothing, Nathan. Your DNA at the scene buries you."

As he opened the door, he was met with a ring of loaded department issued .45 Glocks. Officers of the Tenaple City Police Department screamed at him to get on the ground. Nathan wisely moved to the other corner of the room. If the detective chose not to comply, Nathan didn't want to be the victim of a stray bullet. Detective Johnson took a hesitant step backward, confusion and fear on his face.

"One last thing you should know, Detective," Nathan said. "This interrogation *was* recorded."

Nathan cringed when the officers tackled the suspect and he walked out of the room as they wrestled him under control.

"How?" Detective Johnson managed as he was being cuffed.

Nathan looked over his shoulder at him. "When you have a reputation like mine, all they need is a nod."

The officers forced him out. Captain Stephen Zinger, a tall, heavy-set man with no neck, a balding head, and a sleepy gaze was waiting for him outside. He had long ago traded in his police uniform for the shirt and tie of his rank. Nathan grinned. Zinger shook his head in wonder and disgust.

"If I hadn't seen it with my own eyes, I never would have believed it," he said.

"I only do what's in my job description, Captain."

"Will you stop saying that every time you solve a case? It's pissing me off."

"That's what now? Six?"

"Five. The four-year-old's confession doesn't count."

Nathan breathed a laugh and watched the officers walk the detective to the exit.

"How did you know, Nathan?" Zinger asked.

"When he showed me the photos, he said whoever did it was pissed off. Crimes of passion involving knives are normally repetitive stabbings, not slicing and not like that. He wanted Emily to suffer. It was revenge. Then learning about his wife...it was easy."

"You pressing charges?" Zinger asked.

Nathan shook his head. "Nah. It'd just get dropped, but I *am* going home."

"Just one more thing, Detective. Where is Emily?"

Nathan turned back to the captain. "I'm not a detective anymore, Steve. Santa Fe. Her plane left three hours ago."

"You let her get away?"

"I had to in order to catch this guy."

"But we could have had *her*."

Nathan shook his head again. "She would've killed any officers who tried. You know that. S.W.A.T. can't even handle her."

The captain gave a frustrated nod.

"I'm sorry, Nathan," he said, suddenly. "About Nancy, I mean."

"Wouldn't have happened if I'dda known."

Zinger grunted. "She was brave to agree to something like this."

"Yeah, well, Emily has another body on her conscience. If she even has one."

"You caught the guy, though. Emily's not perfect. She'll make a mistake one day."

Nathan walked toward the exit. "No...she won't."

CHAPTER ONE

———∞∞∞———

MY NAME IS NATHAN MCLAIN. FOUR YEARS AGO I decided I was through with the political bullshit and left my department back in Tennessee to come to the great Tampa Bay. The big city life was just too loud, so I moved to Tenaple – a small town on the outskirts of Clearwater. From the day I arrived here I knew there was something wrong with this place. Maybe it was the air, the ungodly hot, thick air that took over from March to September. Maybe it was the terrible public school system that left next to no hope for our future generations. My personal theory is that the reclaimed water used on everyone's lawns is going airborne and being breathed in to wreak havoc on what little brain capacity there is in the everyday man, and even worse on his future fuck-up of an offspring. The apple doesn't fall far from the tree. Actually, this generation should say the apple *never* falls from the tree, and would rather shrivel up on the branch than roll off on their own. But the kids weren't the worst of them. It was the grown ass adults who gave me migraines. The beaches are beautiful and the women are fine, but there's so much stupid to deal with here. Since leaving, I've found more reasons to question my sanity than my clients'. The grass is always greener my ass. What the *hell* was I thinking?

At least business was booming. People out here don't trust their police, and a lot of them are rich enough, and dumb enough, to pay everything up front just to get an ear. Booming, maybe, but only mildly entertaining. A runaway in a bad neighborhood or a jilted lover. I was even called to find a lost fish once. A lost fish...and the guy *paid* me to tell him that it had probably been swallowed by a seagull. The damn things were everywhere. That's what you get when you put your aquarium outside. But every now and again I'd get a call like the call that changed everything.

Murder.

The scene was in north Pinellas County in a city called Tarpon Springs. Rich town, plenty of mansions, Bentleys, and golf courses. I met the old, rich guy out on his golf course, as a matter of fact. It was his twenty-four year old daughter who was found dead. Single gunshot wound to the head. A cut-and-dry homicide except for one thing: there was no evidence. No exit wound, no bullet in the body, no sign of a struggle, no footprint in the grass. Nothing. Only the "MO" was left behind, carved over the heart of the deceased.

E. H.

Emily Henderson.

This lady was a badass. To this day I've never spoken a word to her. Every time I'm called out for her handy work, there's never a trace of evidence. Just her signature sliced in the same spot. I wasn't too concerned about her at first. Serial killers were police business, but then she crossed the line. Asking *my* girlfriend to cover for her, to take on her identity – I don't think Nancy knew who she was dealing with. She needed money, and Emily exploited that. Now, Nancy's gone. Now, it's personal.

And so, I hunt. I hunt for a scent. If only I knew what she looked like, or even heard her voice. The girl's good. Damn good.

But then, so am I.

CHAPTER TWO

"Ooo, baby, I be stuck to you like glue, baby. Wanna spend it all on you, baby. My room is the g-spot, call me Mr. Flintstone, I can make your bed rock."

The hit single by Young Money and Lloyd rang out as the cell phone vibrated against the night stand. Outdated, maybe, but it was perfect for what he was doing at that moment. Perfect, and yet the meaning behind it was perfectly irritating.

"Nathan," she said between moans in a perfect foreign accent only trumped by her physical beauty, "don't you dare!"

Nathan reached over and checked the screen. Unknown caller. Only one person would be calling at this hour.

"Just let me get him off the phone," Nathan said.

"You're supposed to be getting *me* off," she growled.

The phone was persistent. Nathan planted a kiss on her lips and pressed the answer button on the screen.

"This better be important, Steve," he said, heatedly.

"Why?" came the defiant reply. *"You busy?"*

"Very. Caribbean and French. What the hell are *you* doing up at this hour?"

"I've got a case for you."

"Steve, it's two-thirty and I've got a brunette with double-damns in here."

"A brunette who's about to leave if you don't get off the fucking phone," she chimed in.

"You hear that?"

"Just get here in an hour."

The line went dead.

Nathan put the phone back on the nightstand. *Hour my ass.*

— ✐ —

"ALRIGHT, STEVE," NATHAN SAID. "WHAT'S THE GOD-damned emergency?"

Captain Steven Zinger of the Tenaple City Police Department looked up at him under his eyebrows. Nathan closed the door behind him and approached the captain's desk. He wore faded jeans and a t-shirt with holes in the front. His deep brown hair was unkempt. Jesus, did he climb off the girl, throw on the nearest thing and get in the car? Smooth brows were set in annoyance and his lips were firm. The captain didn't appreciate his short temper.

"I said *one* hour, Nathan."

Nathan pulled out his phone, sliding his finger through the face. Irritation etched into Zinger.

"I'm talking to you, damnit."

Nathan handed him the phone. "Here."

Long brown hair cascaded down her naked body just past her shoulder blades. Her head was turned as she suggestively bit down on the end of a finger. God damn she was beautiful. She knelt on both knees atop his California king-sized bed, her breasts protruding from the thin silk dress with a sleeve slipped down off her shoulder. Her skin tone was a perfect blend of brown and tan.

Shaking his head, Zinger let out a low whistle and grunted as he handed the phone back.

"How did you manage to get *that*?" he asked. "You don't even do your damn hair."

Nathan smiled, turning off the screen put the phone back in his pocket. "I do my hair every day. It looks like this for a reason."

"Do you even know her name?"

"Sonya."

"Did you tell her *your* name?"

Nathan nodded. "And before you called, I was really enjoying the way she was saying it."

The two of them shared a laugh.

"So what's so important, Steve," Nathan pressed, "that you had to take me away from *that?*"

Zinger slid a face down piece of paper across the desk. "Read that."

Nathan's eyes went from the paper to the captain and back before he picked it up. It was a typed document in a small font. The narrative was only half a page long. Steve had read it over so many times he had it memorized.

On 01/07/2013 at 1846 hours, I, Officer Beckman, was dispatched to 3344 Comfort Lane reference an assault incident. The complainant was thirty-two year old Elizabeth Sottrum. Sottrum reported that she was taking her dog for a walk when she heard a shuffling in the bushes next to the sidewalk in front of her home. Sottrum stated that a rabbit jumped out and bit her dog's leg, which snapped it in half. The dog was able to fight off the rabbit, which ran back into the bushes. Sottrum then kicked the bushes to shoo the rabbit out, but it was gone. She alleges that it "just disappeared". Sottrum carried her dog to the vet and had a cast put on the dog's leg. Sottrum immediately called police when she returned home.

Sottrum seemed very alert and responded to my questions promptly.

Nathan looked at Zinger over the paper. "Steve..."

"Why would I bring you here at *this* hour to show you some bullshit? You know me better than that, Nathan"

Nathan lifted the paper with an incredulous look. "Steve, did you read this shit?"

"Several times."

"And you're telling me that you believe a rabbit jumped out of the bushes, snapped a dog's leg in half, jumped back in the bushes, and just *disappeared*? You've been doing this for how long?"

"Long enough to know bullshit when I see it."

"Oh c'mon, Steve! Are you serious?"

Zinger opened a drawer behind the desk. He pulled out four more reports and pushed them over to Nathan.

"These were taken within the week," he said. "Same area."

Nathan read the short narratives one by one. All of them were more absurd than the last. A praying mantis snatching a small Chihuahua. A wolf lurking *in* Comfort Lake. A mouse attacking a young child in the front yard. Nathan shook his head as he read the last narrative.

"The little girl's parents are waiting for you," Zinger added. "I want you to find out what's going on down on Comfort Lane. *I* hope the entire street's on acid."

"Why me?"

"My men have assignments and can't sit on that street all day."

"Bullshit. You don't think they can solve the case."

"I'll tell you what. You figure out what the hell's going on down there, I'll tell the officers that myself."

Nathan lifted the paper with his point. "I hope you don't think I do this just for shits and giggles."

Zinger sighed. "Get out of my office."

NATHAN PULLED IN FRONT OF THE HOUSE, LOOKING AT the number on the mailbox: 3343 Comfort lane. It was a simple one-story brown home with an attached two-car garage. The lone window in the front was covered from inside by dark curtains. Nathan got out and shut the door to his hybrid Toyota, walking up the empty driveway.

"Let's see what this is all about," he mumbled to himself.

His knock was answered promptly by a short blonde-haired woman in her mid-thirties. She was about as wide as she was tall wearing a white shirt and black sweat-pants. Nathan, wondering who would ever get in bed with someone so homely, forced a smile.

"Hello, Mrs...Epson?" he said.

"Yes?"

"I'm Investigator Nathan McLain."

She looked him over, her brows bunching together in doubt. "You're from the police department?" she asked. "Most of the cops I seen are more...professional lookin'."

And she's a bitch, too.

"I understand your daughter was bitten by a mouse?" Nathan asked.

One of the woman's brows rose, but she finally moved to the side. "Come on in."

The door opened up to the living room. A wide flat screen mounted the left wall. Green couches and lazy boys faced the television on a yellowish carpet. Both the coffee and end tables were made of glass. The colors were strange, but the place looked very comfortable.

"Have a seat," Mrs. Epson said, walking towards the hallway next to the television. "Lydia!"

"Yes mommy?" came the cute reply.

"There's someone here to see you."

"Coming."

"Who is it, Honey?" a male voice asked.

"Someone from the police department."

Little Lydia came out first. Her shoulder length blonde hair was brushed back away from her face. She wore a yellow shirt with a Green Bay Packers logo in the center. Nathan suddenly understood the strange color scheme in the living room.

Lydia clung to her mother's clothes in the face of a stranger. Nathan smiled at the girl as he rose from the couch, kneeling down to be on her eye level when he was close enough.

"Hi Lydia," he said.

She shrank back into her mother.

"My name is Nathan."

"Don't be shy, Sweetie," Mrs. Epson said, turning Lydia to face him and holding her daughter's shoulders. "It's alright."

"Hi Nathan," Lydia quietly said.

"I'm from the police department." Nathan put on a sad face. "They told me what happened to you. I came to see if you were okay."

"Thank you." She smiled. The girl was simply adorable. "I'm okay. I got bit by a mousy."

"The doctor said she didn't have rabies or anything," Mrs. Epson said from above.

"Can you show me where the mousy bit you?" Nathan asked.

Lydia turned her left arm to show him the back of her triceps. The small teeth marks were scabbed over and looked to be very deep. Not a typical mouse bite, Nathan knew.

"That must have hurt," Nathan said.

Lydia nodded as she lowered her arm. "Uh huh. I didn't cry, though."

"You didn't?"

"Uh uh."

"You are a brave girl. I think I would have cried if a mousy bit me."

She grinned. "I'm a big girl."

"Yes you are. Can you tell me how old you are?"

Lydia held up a hand. "Five."

Nathan smiled. "Very good."

Heavy steps approached from the hall. A big man, looking like a mountain compared to the rest of his family, emerged. Compared to her husband, Mrs. Epson was like Sonya.

Nathan stood and offered a hand. "Nathan McLain."

"Andrew Epson," the man replied. "Is everything alright?"

Nathan nodded. "I just came by to check on Lydia and find out what happened."

"Why don't we all sit down and get away from this hallway."

"Actually, I don't plan on being here that long. Lydia," Nathan knelt again, "I know it might be scary, but do you think you can show me where you were playing when the mousy bit you?"

Lydia adamantly nodded. "Uh huh, I was in the front."

She darted past him to the door and scurried into the yard.

"I was playing with Courtney here," she said.

"Courtney?" Nathan asked.

"Her doll," Mrs. Epson explained.

"Did you see what the mousy looked like, Lydia?"

Lydia's hair swished back and forth as she shook her head. "I just felt it bite me."

"What happened after it bit you?"

She pointed to the young tree decorating the corner of the property. "It ran over there."

Nathan walked around the yard until he reached the tree. There was no hole or anything that the mouse could come out of. Something blue caught his eye. He squatted and shined the small flashlight on his keys where the trunk met the dirt. A spot of blue residue about the size of his fist glowed at the base of the tree. Nathan scowled. He didn't know any substance that glowed like that.

"Did you find something?" Mr. Epson called.

"Just some droppings," Nathan said.

He pulled out a plastic bag and a pair of latex gloves from his pocket. He cautiously touched the blue residue to see if it was corrosive. Finding it safe, Nathan collected up a handful of ground and dumped it into the bag, adding his gloves in with it before sealing it up and putting it back in his pocket. He then walked back to the family.

Lydia had gone back inside, leaving her parents at the doorway.

"Thank you for your time, Mister and Missus Epson." Nathan fished out a business card for the police department. "Please call if you need anything."

He looked at the bag before placing it in the front passenger seat. His cell phone buzzed with the arrival of a text message. Another picture from Sonya. Appealing as it was, he wasn't interested. A mystery had just taken form. Zinger would want to know about this.

⸺ ◦◦◦ ⸺

ZINGER SCRUTINIZED THE BAGGIE OF GROUND.

"I don't see anything," he said.

"Trust me," Nathan replied, "it's in there."

"Any idea of what it could be?"

Nathan shrugged. "*I've* never seen anything like it before."

"You said it was...glowing?"

"You know me, Steve. Would I ever exaggerate?"

Zinger chuckled as he placed the bag back atop his desk. "No, I suppose not. I'll have Forensics take a look at it."

"Great."

"Where are you going?"

"Home." Nathan turned back from the doorway. "I've got to be somewhere for lunch tomorrow – well, *today* – and you're hell bent on keeping me up all night."

Zinger lifted a brow. "Another date?"

A smile tugged on the corner of Nathan's mouth. "I don't go on dates anymore, Steve."

Zinger stifled a laugh and shook his head. "Get out of my office."

———

THE HYBRID ENGINE CAME ON WITH A WHISPER. HIS ON deck system booted up, lighting the screen in the middle of his dashboard. He plugged in his phone to the USB auxiliary port in the center console before putting on his seat belt and backing out of the parking spot. The sun shined brightly in the early afternoon. The lunch hour had passed, so the downtown area was basically traffic-free. He headed toward the causeway. The sun glistened off the water, seeming to follow him as he drove.

The hotel-restaurant with the pavilion overlooking the bay rose slowly in the distance. As he passed the entrance he saw her standing alone with her hands against the wooden beam.

"I didn't think you got my text," she said as he wrapped his arms around her from behind.

"I wouldn't miss a chance to see you," Nathan replied.

"Is it too much to ask for a reply?"

"I really hope you didn't bring me here to fight with me."

She sighed and leaned her head back against his shoulder. "Of course not. I'm sorry. I've had a rough day."

Nathan slid his hand up the waist of her silky white blouse. The gray slacks she wore hugged the curves she pressed back against him. Long, dirty-blond hair that she always wore down tickled his cheek. She made an approving sound in her throat as he gently groped the large protruding mounds that were her breasts. They pressed against him when she suddenly whirled and wrapped her arms around him. Her black square-framed glasses that pronounced her hazel eyes sat perfectly on the bridge of her nose. Soft, pouty lips met his in a passionate kiss, her hand running up the back of his head. She was lean in frame; tall and perfectly built from her daily workouts. Nathan pulled her middle against him as he returned the kiss. Slowly, breathlessly, she pulled back, her tongue sliding against his bottom lip.

"I'm not hungry all of a sudden," she said, pulling her lip into her teeth.

Nathan looked around at the pavilion speckled with couples gazing out at the shimmering water.

"I'm waiting for a call," he replied, refocusing on her.

Her annoyance returned and she leaned away from him. "*Seriously?*"

"I got a case this morning."

"What the fuck, Nathan."

Nathan shushed her. "What do you want from me? I have to make money."

"This was supposed to be *our* day."

"I thought I'd have it off after the last case."

She sighed in return and looked away. "Just *one* day. I'd like just *one* day where we can sit and enjoy a lunch without you running off."

"I said I'm waiting on a call, Candice. I didn't say we couldn't eat."

"And what's going to happen if you get the call during our lunch? You gonna run off on your case?"

"It depends on what the call says."

Candice pushed away from him with a sigh and started walking away. Nathan took her arm before she walked past.

"Candice..."

"I took time off for this, Nathan," she seethed through gritted teeth.

"Candice, you know what I do. The way I see it we can spend the time here fighting or we can make the most of the time we have."

She sighed, but still didn't look at him.

"C'mon, babe. I'm here; you know I want to spend time with you."

"Only if you can follow directions."

"Excuse me?"

She gave him a sidelong glance. "I'm not hungry anymore. I'll only stay here if you can follow directions."

"Candice..."

"If the phone rings, you can answer it. I know you have to, but until then you're mine."

A mischievous smile crept onto her face.

"We can't go too far," Nathan said.

"My place, then?"

Nathan shook his head. "Too far away."

She pouted playfully. "I have a taste for chocolate strawberries."

Nathan's pants immediately became tight.

"If we go back to your place," he started, "you're going to be late getting back to work."

One final kiss from her soft lips burned away all resolve. Her hand, interlocked with his, guided him to his car – she always took a taxi. She was already working

18

his zipper as he shifted the car into reverse. Typical Candice, always knowing exactly what to say to get what she wanted. He had a difficult time focusing as he drove, having to force his eyelids open and adjust his blurry vision several times. He gripped the steering wheel as her head bobbed and he did his best to keep consistent pressure on the gas.

He finally found a spot in the parking garage under her apartment. Her arm reached across his lap. His chair made a buzzing sound as it slowly tilted backward. She was not even looking. Impressive.

When the buzzing stopped, she came up and kissed him.

"You just relax. I'll take care of the first one."

And just as she started working her hips against him, his phone buzzed.

———— ∞ ————

NATHAN WALKED INTO ZINGER'S OFFICE, GIVING HIS best Lurch impression from the Addam's Family. "You called?"

Zinger looked up from a paper he was reading. "It's 'you *rang*.'"

"Actually, it depends on the sound that comes out when the rope is pulled."

Zinger looked back down to the paper. His demeanor told Nathan something wasn't right.

"What'chu got, Steve?"

"Remember the little girl you saw yesterday?"

Nathan nodded. "Lydia. What about her?"

Zinger slid the paper he was reading across the desk. When Nathan read the headline, his jaw dropped.

"No way," he whispered. "I just saw her yesterday. She was fine."

"Well, she's not now," Zinger said.

Nathan looked up at him. "When?"

"The 9-1-1 call was placed at lunchtime."

"Why didn't you call me before now?"

Zinger lifted a brow. "I called you as soon as we got confirmation from the hospital. They...couldn't tell if it was her."

The captain opened a manila folder atop his desk and slid an enlarged photo over to Nathan.

"That can't be her," Nathan said.

"DNA confirms it," Zinger replied.

Nathan picked up the photo of the young girl's face and shoulders. The full blonde hair he saw yesterday was now thin and disheveled. Lydia's small face was decayed and plagued with pock marks, abrasions, and sickening splits along her forehead. Her lips were gnarled and eaten back, showing a mouth of rotten teeth. It was like she had died from some sort of disease.

Nathan shook his head. "There's no way, Steve. I saw this girl yesterday. She was normal. She even showed me where she was attacked."

Zinger slid another photo of the girl's arm across the desk.

"The doctors say that was where this all started," he added.

"This is impossible."

"The family's still at the General Hospital. Go see for yourself."

MR. EPSON HAD BOTH ARMS AROUND HIS BLANK LOOKING wife, rocking her back and forth as they sat together in the hospital waiting room. Nathan sighed through his nose. He hated this part. The family had enough to deal with knowing their daughter was dead. Now he had to ask all these questions.

Mr. Epson saw him first and whispered something to his wife. She leaned forward, allowing him to stand up, but continued to stare ahead at nothing. Nathan stopped a ways off when he saw Mr. Epson approaching.

"Nathan," he said.

"Mr. Epson." Nathan hesitated, shaking his head. "I'm sorry for your loss."

"Thank you." He searched for words. "I just wish I understood how this happened. She seemed just fine yesterday."

"I know. I need to ask a couple questions. Do you think you can talk about this now?"

"*I* can, but," Mr. Epson turned and looked at his wife, "I don't think she'll be ready for a while. What do you need to know?"

"What happened after I left?"

Mr. Epson sighed as he placed a hand on his hip and ran the other through his unkempt brown hair. "Uh, nothing unusual. We went to bed, got up, ate breakfast, went to the park. I put Lydia down for a nap and when I went to wake her she was..."

"Did Lydia ever complain of pain or discomfort? Or *anything?*"

"She said the bite marks hurt when she touched them, but that's not unusual."

"That's all? Nothing else?"

Mr. Epson shook his head. "No. She said it tingled, but that's not unusual either."

"Is there anything else? Was she acting strange or do anything that you thought was unlike her?"

Again, Mr. Epson shook his head. "No. Lydia was herself; down to the complaints about having to take a nap."

Nathan pressed his lips together and thanked Mr. Epson for his time. He pushed the hospital doors open and went to the front desk. A nurse, dressed in the dark green scrubs of her profession sat behind it. Her brown hair was tied in a doughnut behind her head. She looked up as he approached. Big green eyes captivated him through small dark glasses that matched her head perfectly. Her small nose pointed over full, pouty lips and a cleft chin.

Nathan almost swallowed his tongue. Of all the times he had been to the hospital he had never seen this beauty before.

"Can I help you with something, sir?" she asked, her voice as beautiful as the rest of her.

Nathan cleared his throat. "I was wondering if I could see Lydia."

"Oh, are you an officer?"

"Yes."

"Okay." She pointed down the open hall to his left. "I think the police are still outside her door. It's just down the hall. Would you mind signing in?"

"Thank you, Miss...?"

"Joy," she said with a smile.

"Thank you Miss Joy."

"Just Joy is fine. And you are?"

"Nathan McLain. Investigator Nathan McLain."

He reached across the desk and gently shook her small hand.

"Ooo...*Investigator?*" she lowered her voice. "Is there a crime here?"

Nathan winked at her. "Sorry, Joy. If I told you, I'd have to kill you."

Joy's laughter followed him as he walked on. It was in terrible spirits perhaps, flirting while investigating the death of a young girl, but she was too beautiful not to make the attempt. Young, gorgeous, not a chance he'd walk by that without a 'hello'.

Two officers casually stood outside the closed door. When they saw him, they lifted brows of mild interest. The officers were not very fond of his reputation among the department. His status pushed theirs further under foot.

Nathan said nothing to them and gently rapped on the door.

"Who is it?"

"Nathan McLain."

The handle flicked and the door inched open. The body lay in bed with a sheet over it. A bald doctor stood over her, speaking in hushed tones with a tall man in a dark blue suit, one arm folded under the elbow of the other as he held his chin with his hand. He introduced Nathan without looking at him.

"Dr. Stein, Nathan McLain. He's working this case with us."

Nathan flipped a hand in greeting, which the doctor returned with a nod.

"What do we got, Stan?" Nathan asked.

Detective Stan McIntosh shrugged his broad shoulders as he scowled down at the body. He pressed his lips together.

"Your guess is as good as mine," he said in a deep voice. "Have you seen the body yet?"

"Only photos," Nathan replied. "But I saw the girl yesterday. She was fine—"

Detective McIntosh motioned him over and lifted the sheet. Nathan winced. The girl looked worse than she did in the photos.

"This is what she looks like now," the detective said.

"What's COD?" Nathan asked.

Both men looked over at him shaking their heads.

"One day she's fine," Detective McIntosh said, slightly lifting the sheet in his hand. "The next..."

Nathan shook his head as he looked down at the gnarled body. The poor little girl...

"Do we have *anything* at all?" he asked.

"Actually, yes," Dr. Stein said.

Detective McIntosh pulled back the sheet to show the girl's face. Dr. Stein pulled out a small flashlight and pressed a button as he pointed it at the body. Something illuminated under the black light across Lydia's face. Nathan scowled. It looked exactly the same as the blue dirt he found.

"What is it?" he asked.

"Forensics took a sample to find out," Detective McIntosh said.

"It's nothing I recognize," Dr. Stein added.

No shit, Sherlock.

"How long are you going to be here?" Nathan asked the detective.

"Hard to say. Hour at least."

Nathan turned and strode to the door. "I'll call you."

"Likewise."

Nathan had worked with the agency long enough to build a rapport with the detectives, if not the patrolmen. This was no longer a pissing match between investigator and police. A little girl had died.

———— ∞ ————

"NATHAN, HOW MANY TIMES DO I HAVE TO TELL YOU that you need special clearance to be in this area?"

"Really, Shellie," Nathan replied, approaching from behind. "We got a dead girl and you're worried about my special clearance."

"Ah, the good old guilt trip. A tactic you use often, and always, to get what you want."

Nathan stopped next to her and looked up at the computer screen atop the desk.

"And it works every time," he added. "What are we looking at?"

"This is a magnified comparison between the blue dirt you gave me and whatever's all over Lydia."

Nathan narrowed his eyes at the screen. "So I take it you haven't figured it out, yet?"

The ponytail of Shellie Durnan's long, dark hair swished out behind her and she whirled and walked to another computer desk. The white lab coat she wore caught stray hairs at her shoulders and back. Her heels clicked against the smooth tile floor. Though she worked in a lab, the woman swore by her slacks and blouses.

"Don't I always figure it out, Nathan?" she said in annoyance.

"This is why I keep sending you shit, Shellie. If you don't want to see me anymore, stop doing such a good job."

Shellie fiddled with the mouse. "Flattery will get you nowhere."

Shellie was of average build, what she called "a few extra pounds on the side". Nathan always thought the woman had the body for softball. Fine brows bunched in concentration over her dark eyes. The bridge of her small nose protruded out rather than curving in and her wide mouth seemed to always have a sarcastic smirk. For anyone who knew her, the smirk foreshadowed the woman's personality.

"So?" Nathan pressed.

"The blue dirt and the substance on Lydia's face are a perfect match."

"A match for?"

Shellie pressed down on the mouse and a printer immediately began its noisy task.

"I don't know," she replied.

Nathan sighed. "You know, you're really starting to fall on my list of experts."

"It's kind of difficult to test a substance that disappears by the millisecond."

Nathan blinked. "What?"

Shellie looked over at him. "The bag you gave me? There was maybe a fingernail's length of blue substance left, and even that was gone in seconds."

"It disappeared?"

"Yeah. And I'm not The Flash. Neither is any of my equipment, for that matter."

"What about the sample from Lydia's face?"

Shellie shook her head. "Gone." She pointed toward the big screen. "Those are photos."

"Any idea at all of what we're dealing with here? You know, 'based on your training and experience'?"

"*In my expert opinion*, I think it's either some sort of radioactive fungus or bacteria. I'll need another sample, preferably one that lasts longer than five minutes."

Nathan pulled out his phone. As he pressed the home button, the phone rang. Detective McIntosh.

"Is that *seriously* your *ring*tone?" Shellie scoffed.

"I make magic happen to this song."

"Oho God!"

Nathan pressed on the screen. "I'll take a wild guess: the blue stuff's all gone."

"*How'd you know?*"

Nathan sighed. "I'll be there in twenty."

"ALRIGHT BOYS, WHAT DO WE GOT?"

Nathan and Detective McIntosh shared a sidelong glance, mentally asking each other who was going to answer the Captain first.

"We don't really know, sir," the detective replied.

"What do you mean 'you don't really know'?" Captain Zinger asked. "What did Forensics say?"

"Shellie thinks it's a radioactive fungus or bacteria," Nathan explained.

"She *thinks*?"

"Apparently, it has a half-life of about twenty seconds."

The Captain grunted. "That explains why I didn't see it in the bag." He let out a sigh through his nose.

"So what now?" McIntosh asked.

"We wait for another report," Zinger said.

"What about Lydia?"

"Whatever killed her is completely gone, apparently. I imagine Forensics will let us know if they find something. Let's hope this blue shit doesn't become an epidemic."

"I'm going to go talk to the family again."

The Detective saluted the Captain and walked out of his office.

"What's on your mind, Detective?" Captain Zinger asked when Nathan didn't move.

"Something's not right, here, Steve. I saw that girl yesterday and she was completely fine. She didn't even have an issue going to the spot where she was attacked." Nathan shook his head and looked off, recalling the memory of Lydia in her hospital bed. "She was completely healthy. Then the next day she dies from this stuff and it just *disappears*? I don't like it."

"What are you thinking?"

"We might be dealing with something *else*."

"Something else as in...?"

Nathan shook his head again. "I'm not sure, yet." He turned toward the door. "I'll let you know what I come up with."

"Nathan."

He looked back at the Captain.

"Stay on your toes."

Nathan smiled. "Are you worried about me, Steve?"

"Get out of my office."

NATHAN CLOSED THE DOOR BEHIND HIM AND TOSSED the keys on the table. Two eyes glowed from the shadows of the dim lighting. An instant later, they rushed to him. Nathan braced, the form coming too quick for him to prepare. A tongue attacked his face as his year-old husky jumped into him. He patted the dog's head.

"You know you're not supposed to jump on people, Butch," he said, pushing the dog's paws to the ground. "I didn't spend a buck fifty for you to ignore your training."

He flipped on a light. Boxes lined the floor in the living room, only the couch having any freedom. All of them full of Nancy's things he had managed to collect together throughout the weeks. Sometimes he couldn't bring himself to look for another piece of their relationship. The memory of her was still a fresh wound, no matter how many girls he dated.

Butch ran through the labyrinth, whining when he ran into a box. Nathan tossed his coat on the small table with his keys and walked to the short hallway leading to his room. Butch forced his way into the room first, brushing against Nathan's leg. His bed was unkempt; several boxes lined the foot of it. He walked to the far wall where his computer light flickered in its hibernated state.

Nathan jostled the mouse, sitting in the chair at the desk. The computer's fan kicked on and the screen brightened the dark room. Windows of several newspaper headlines popped up on the screen. He clicked from one paper to the next, the headlines to the articles burning permanently into his mind. "Tenaple's Own Murders in Cold Blood," "Young Girl Murdered, Criminal Behind Bars," "Detective Brutally Murders". Nathan read the articles, one by one. And one by one, they all missed the *real* story.

His eyes went to the framed photo next to the display screen. A couple in love looked back at him. His heart skipped a beat as he studied her, from her brunette hair tied back behind her head to the freckles flecked around her cheeks and nose. Her eyes held so much. So much vigor. So much hope. Love. *Life*. He swallowed at the lump that was rising in his throat.

Nathan forced his eyes back to the screen. He searched all major news sites in Santa Fe, looking for a clue. Any clue. A recent murder, a missing person. Nothing came up. Not a god-damned thing. Nathan put his head in his hand and shut his eyes. A nuzzle at his side brought him out of it. Butch looked up with two different colored eyes, one amber and one blue. His nostrils flared as he sniffed. Nathan patted his pet's black head and lowered his forehead to the dog's. Butch yanked his head away and darted off, content. That was Butch's way; show concern and once he knew Nathan was okay, he went on to the next interesting thing. Which was usually one of the million balls that were scattered throughout the apartment, in various stages of destruction. Nathan allowed himself to smile as Butch brought one back in. He turned in a circle and laid down with a grunt, using a paw to steady the tennis ball as he worked on chewing off the skin, yet he still watched Nathan in his chair.

Nathan looked to the computer again, then drifted up to the clippings of newspaper he hand taped to the wall behind his display screen. The articles covered all of Emily Henderson's murders. Now she was gone. Without a trace. And he'd allowed her to go in order to catch the detective. He often wondered if he had traded in the golden goose for a rooster.

With a sigh, he shut down the computer and rose from the seat. The alarm clock next to his bed read a quarter to midnight. He had come home after nine. He didn't realize he had spent that much time looking for her. Nathan stripped down to his boxers and climbed into bed, taking a moment to plug in his phone. His thoughts shifted to the blue substance he had found. He wondered what it could be. Where was it even coming from? If it was so erosive, why didn't it burn through the plastic bag he had put it in, or the glove? Hopefully Shellie found something. He began to drift off to sleep, his thoughts settling on Nancy. He could still smell her in the pillow. God he would have given anything to hold her right now. Even in his dreams.

Just as his dreams were becoming a slumberous reality, his phone rang. He looked at the name and quickly answered it.

"Hello?"

"Oh I'm sorry," the voice said. *"Did I wake you?"*

"No, no. I'm just tired."

"I'm sorry. I saw you called earlier. I'm just getting off work."

"Yeah, I figured you were working."

"What are you up to?"

"I'm already in bed. Why?"

"I had a long day and I'm hungry. I'm considering going to Thane's."

Nathan looked at the clock. It wasn't like he had a client to see tomorrow. The Lydia case was waiting on something from Shellie. He had some investigation to do, but nothing that needed immediate attention. Besides, he was dying to see what she looked like outside her work clothes.

"Alright. I'll meet you there."

THE SPORTS BAR WAS BASICALLY ABANDONED. IN THE final two hours to closing on a Monday night, that wasn't unusual. The few groups of people were more absorbed in the televisions hanging around the place than each other. Nathan had forgotten about March Madness. The University of Florida had a high chance to win it all.

She came in and spotted him, smiling and giving him a wave as she headed over. Her jeans hugged her legs and her black jacket fit her lean frame. Though she had on a couple layers to protect her from the late-night chill, her breasts refused to be ignored.

"Ugh, I'm starving," she said, sitting in the booth across from him.

"When was the last time you ate?"

She shook her head as she took off her jacket and placed it in the booth next to her. Her shirt did everything to show off her endowments. "I don't even remember anymore. It's been go, go, go all day. Maybe at noon."

Nathan checked his phone. "How are you still on your feet? I'd have eaten one of the patients."

She giggled. "I was so busy I didn't have time to think about it."

"Well, good thing I'm here. Meals are always better when they're free."

The waitress came around and took their drink orders, sliding menus down on the table. Joy eagerly picked one up.

"You don't have to pay, you know," she said.

"You've had a long day. This one's on me."

She resigned without much protest. "I'm normally not this easy on dates."

"Oh this isn't a date," Nathan said.

"It's not?"

"No. If this was a date, we wouldn't be dressed in jeans. The food would be much more expensive. There would be a view, and I would smell fantastic."

She giggled. "I gotta say I've never looked this...simple on a date before. So what is this, then?"

He shrugged. "A couple of adults having a casual night out. I mean, c'mon." He gestured to the restaurant with a hand. "A date at a Sports Bar? We're not college kids."

"I wouldn't expect much else at this hour."

"We'll have to meet up earlier, then. When's your next day off?"

"Wednesday, but I only work until eight tomorrow. Don't you have a client?"

Nathan winked. "I make time for special occasions."

Blush touched her cheeks as she smiled at him.

"It's a date then," she said. "A *real* date."

"I'll let you know where we're going tomorrow."

"You mean you don't know?"

"I have a few places. Depends on how special I want to make this."

"Well, I look much different outside my casual clothes. I don't want to feel overdressed."

The waitress returned with their drinks. A wide margarita glass was placed in front of her, a draft Miller Fortune for him.

"Is there any food you don't like?" Nathan asked.

"I love sushi."

"I don't know anyone who *doesn't* love sushi."

The night went on. They spoke about their interests and dislikes, the crazy things they observed about people and how shitty it was to work with them. They ordered another round as the conversation jumped from topic to topic. All in all, it was a great night, just what Nathan needed.

As he walked her to her car, a chill overcame him. His eyes went to the shadows, but nothing was there. He dismissed the feeling. Probably the alcohol.

"If this was a date, I'd tell you that I had a great time tonight," Joy said.

"And I'd offer for us to go out again," Nathan said.

"Too bad. I might have said yes."

They reached her two-door Honda Civic. The lights flashed as she remotely unlocked the doors. She turned to him before getting in.

"So...now what?"

"I guess we start at the beginning. Will you go out with me?"

She smiled. "I'd love to."

The streetlight above cast her in an orange glow. Maybe it was her beauty combined with the alcohol.

Maybe it was his fluttering insides, but something told him not to let her get away yet. He wrapped his arms around her waist and pulled her in gently. She didn't fight him as their faces drew close. A finger pressed against his lips, stopping them before they met hers.

"This isn't a date, remember?" she whispered.

Why the fuck did he ever say that?

She gently pulled away from him, her coy smile retreating. She finally broke eye contact and got into her car. He stepped back enough to allow her to back out of the parking space. She looked at him one last time, giving him a wave before pulling out of the parking lot. He stood there, watching her go. Her car merged into traffic and disappeared down the road.

She consumed his mind as he walked back to his car. He could still smell her, still feel her in his arms. She felt good. Soft. She wasn't as pretty as Sonya, or even Candice, yet she was somehow more attractive to him than either of the two. He thought about how she toyed with him. Firm, yet playful. She was a rare one. A smile crept onto his face.

Let the games begin.

CHAPTER THREE

———⌘———

RED AND BLUE FLASHED AGAINST THE HOUSES ON COM-
fort Lane. Nathan pulled up behind a dark police cruiser
and climbed out of the car. Several officers in their dark
blue uniforms stood in the driveway of a corner lot. The
early morning air bit his unprotected skin as he walked.
He cursed himself for not thinking enough to wear
sleeves, or at least bring a jacket. Nathan searched the
men in blue until he picked out the night supervisor,
Sergeant Christopher Wells. This was *not* how he had
planned to spend his Tuesday night.

"Do you need us?" one of the officers asked.

Sergeant Wells gave a quick shake of his head. "Nah,
I should be alright." He looked at Nathan as the officers
went back to their cruisers to leave the scene. "*You* look
like hell."

Nathan glared at the sergeant as he walked up. "What
do you expect at four-thirty?"

Wells shrugged with a smirk. "From what I hear, you
really don't have much better to do."

It took Nathan a moment to get what the sergeant was referring to. He couldn't stop the smile from crawling onto his face and he dug his cell out of his phone. "You want to see her?"

"*Hell* yes," Wells replied. "What was she? Bolivian and French?"

"*Caribbean* and French."

Wells made an approving sound in his throat as Nathan handed over his phone. He shook his head as his gaze lingered on her body. "How did you get her to pose like that?"

"I came out of the bathroom and there she was. She actually told me to take the picture. Something about always remembering her or something."

Wells' eyes came up. "Do you?"

Nathan nodded slowly, making a few sounds of his own before looking to the house.

Sergeant Christopher Wells was a heavily muscled man. Standing only up to Nathan's shoulders earned him the nickname "Mammoth Midget" throughout the department. His dark hair was cut short and spiked with gel. Sharp features and beady eyes gave Wells an intimidating, raptor-like gaze. He always looked a moment away from exploding on whatever his eyes settled on. The man was competent, though. His hard-nosed drive and flawless reputation had earned respect with Nathan. If Wells was on the case, it was pretty much open and shut.

"So what do we got here?" Nathan asked.

The sergeant snapped back to the issue at hand. His voice was solemn and firm. "The complainant said she saw something strange in the back shed."

Irritation etched into Nathan. "You couldn't have told me about that tomorrow?"

"Police files are confidential."

"Police *reports* are public record. You...*were* going to write a report, weren't you? It's kind of part of your job."

Wells chuckled. "Fuck you, *Detective.*"

Nathan looked over at the sergeant, adding a bit of solemnness to his own voice. "What's going on, Em and Em?"

Wells began walking up the driveway. "This is another one of those crazy reports. This lady said she saw some glowing eyes in the shed. Zinger told me to call you with shit like this."

Nathan was bewildered. "He told you to call *me*? Why wouldn't *he* take the call? *He's* the captain."

Wells looked over with a smirk. "You're not with us. All you have to say is no."

Nathan scowled at Wells. He knew *damn* well Nathan wasn't going to say no.

Sergeant Wells didn't even knock on the door, instead turning the knob and pushing it open. A couple waited for them at the back glass doors across the room. Both were blond-haired and shaped like gourds. The man was taller with a well-kempt beard and mustache. Though the woman was wide, her long bangs framed strikingly attractive features. Even at this early hour, she had a touch of blush on her cheeks and glossy lips. They might have been heavy-set, but they were not an unattractive couple.

Sergeant Wells leaned over, whispering to Nathan as they approached.

"Evening mister and missus Johnson," Nathan said. "I'm Nathan McLain. I understand something strange happened tonight?"

Missus Johnson nodded, causing her hair to swish. "Yes," she said in a heavy southern drawl. She turned, allowing Nathan to see through the glass door behind her and pointed a thumb. "Out back. I woke up and came down ta the kitchen to get a drank and I saw that the shed was open. I figured Thomas had just forgot ta lock it, but when I went out there I heard a funneh sound. Like a...chewin' or somethin'." She shrugged. "I thought it was a mouse. Thomas eats out there sometimes when he's workin' in the yard. When I opened the shed, I saw two big blue eyes lookin' back at meh. A *glowin'* blue. Like somethin' out a horror movie. Boy, I slammed the door shut and got the heck outta there. I didn't even lock it, neither. I heard all about that Lydia girl. That ain't 'bout ta happen to me. No sir!"

"Did you see what it was?" Nathan asked.

She shook her head again. "Once I saw them eyes, I took off. Screamin' fer Thomas. I'm surprised I ain't wake up the whole neighborhood. Then I called ya'll, right away!"

Nathan and Wells shared a look. If the creature was still in there, it was a good chance to break open the case.

"Mind if we take a look?" Nathan asked.

"Be our guest," Mister Johnson said. He cleared his throat when his words came out grated. He had obviously recently woken from sleep.

"Just be careful," his wife added. "Don't get bit."

Nathan and Wells stepped out into the backyard. The dark shed stood in the far corner just before meeting the fence, one of its doors standing open. Nathan took a deep breath.

"Stay sharp," he said.

"Always," Wells said, flicking on his flashlight.

The two cautiously made their way toward the shed, a slight breeze chilling his arms. Nathan's heart hammered in his chest as he stepped off the back porch and onto the grass. He kept his eyes active and his head on a swivel. With the door open, the mouse could have easily ran out and be anywhere in the yard. Wells lit the way ahead, the light giving them limited visibility. Dark blades of grass turned a forest green when hit by the intense LEDs, reflecting some off their surfaces.

Halfway to the shed, a screech stole their attention to the left. Wells hit it with the light just as it went airborne. Glowing blue eyes and sharp teeth dove at Nathan.

"Shit!"

He was just able to duck out of the way. A heavy thud and a rustle of small feet brought the eyes back up. It recovered quickly, diving for a leg. Nathan snatched his foot back, the teeth narrowly missing. Once again it disappeared into the shadows. Wells couldn't keep up with the creature's movement. It was fast. *Too* fast to be anything Nathan had ever seen.

Wells frantically searched with his flashlight. Apprehension tingled Nathan's skin. The thing had been after *him*. Images of Lydia's decayed body flashed through his mind. She had been bitten by something like this. If he couldn't find it...

As he retreated a step to get closer to Wells, the screech came again. Nathan turned to see the eyes coming at him. With his weight on his back foot, he had no chance to dodge. Instinctively, his arm came up to protect his face. He turned, leaning away as he braced for the pain he knew was coming.

A single shot thundered in the night air.

Nathan, his eyes squeezing shut, slammed against the ground. Pain exploded into his shoulder. The other pain never came. His heavy breathing overcame the ringing in his ears. Nathan quickly looked up over his shoulder. Wells was holstering his sidearm with one hand, using the other to light up the creature as he approached. It lay on its side, its chest still rising and falling with rapid breaths. Nathan scrambled to his feet.

"What is it?" he called.

"Looks like a raccoon," Wells replied.

"It didn't sound like a raccoon."

He caught up to Wells and bent at the waist to look at it. It *was* a raccoon, down to the stripes on its tail. Its breathing became raspy as it sucked at the air. Its eyelids drooped over illuminated blue eyes. The glowing iris consumed where the pupil would have been. Finally, the raccoon took its last breath and its chest stilled. From the gunshot wound on its side, a shining blue haze suddenly wafted up.

"Whoa," Wells said as he and Nathan took several steps back.

It only lasted a few seconds and the night was normal again. Nathan shared another look with the sergeant, his flashlight still on the dead animal.

"What was *that*?" Wells asked.

Nathan shook his head.

The sound of the glass door sliding broke the silence. "Are ya'll alright?" came Missus Johnson's voice.

"Yeah, we're fine," Nathan answered over his shoulder. He looked at Wells. "You have an evidence bag?"

"Of course."

"We'll need it. Bring several." Nathan looked at the raccoon. "I don't want its blood getting on us."

"Good news," Nathan said when they reached the house. "We found the mouse."

"Was it...?" was all Missus Johnson could manage to say.

Nathan shook his head as the sergeant walked past them. "No, it was actually a raccoon. We had to kill it."

"With a gun?" Mister Johnson asked suspiciously.

"It was already dying," Nathan explained. "We just put it out of its misery. Possibly rabid."

"What about the blue eyes?" Missus Johnson asked.

Nathan shrugged. "Maybe it was the reflection from the moonlight. I've seen that with my dog before. Scares the bahjesus out of me."

"Are you sure?" Missus Johnson asked, looking out the back glass nervously.

He waved a hand in the air. "Oh yeah. You've got nothing to worry about."

The sergeant came back a short time later with several large brown paper bags. He tossed Nathan a pair of latex gloves and opened the sliding glass door.

"What's that for?" Mister Johnson asked.

"Police protocol," Nathan replied. "We have to show the evidence of what the sergeant here shot at. Besides, you wouldn't want vultures in your yard, would you?"

"*Hell* no," Mister Johnson said with finality.

Nathan chuckled as he headed out to the yard, closing the door behind him.

"Police protocol?" the sergeant asked when he was close enough.

"You got a better excuse? Don't touch it with the glove. Use the bag."

The sergeant's incredulous face turned up to Nathan.

"You heard about the girl who died, right? I was with her the day before. She was completely fine. I don't know what we're dealing with, here. I'd rather be safe."

Wells shook his head as he tore one of the bags, using it as an extra barrier to carefully scoop the raccoon into the other bag. He rolled the top of the bag over and placed it in another before handing it to Nathan, who was already on the phone with Shellie.

"This better be fucking good," came her tired, annoyed *voice.*

"I've got a sample for you. Freshly killed."

"You KILLED one?!"

"The thing almost killed *me*. Em and Em killed it."

Shellie grunted. *"Damn shame. The world would have been better off."*

Nathan hung up the phone and held the top of the bag in a fist.

"Thank you, officers," Missus Johnson said as they were walked out the front door.

"Anytime, ma'am," Wells replied. "If anything else like this happens, make sure you don't try to do it on your own."

"Oh you don't have to worry 'bout that. Take care, now."

Nathan's heart pounded with newfound excitement as they walked down the driveway. This could be the first big break in the case. If they were going to figure out what it was he had to act fast.

"What's with you?" came Wells' question when Nathan began jogging.

"I've got to get this stuff to the lab," Nathan explained.

"You act like it's about to close or something. They won't even look at it until tomorrow."

"Shellie's going in," he said over his shoulder, nearly sprinting to his car. "I need an escort."

"WELL?"

"Nathan...get out."

"Have you figured out what it is yet?"

Shellie whirled in her computer chair. Her hair was tied back in a loose ponytail and her lab coat covered her pink pajamas with Tweety birds on them. Her eyes were bloodshot. He could see the muscles in her jaw flex.

"Nathan," she hissed through gritted teeth, "wait out in the lobby."

Nathan wisely lifted his hands defensively before pushing through the swinging door and walking down the hallway to the lobby. Captain Zinger and Sergeant Wells spoke in hushed tones by the vending machines in a sectioned off part of the room. Zinger saw Nathan over Wells' shoulder.

"Did she kick you out?" he called across the room.

Nathan nodded, approaching them.

"Still working on it?" the captain continued.

"*That* and she's still pissed that I woke her up."

"She understands why you did, though...right?"

Nathan nodded again, stopping a couple steps away. "Yeah. Time's ticking."

"I've gotta get back on the street," Sergeant Wells said, looking to Zinger. "If I get any other calls like this I'll let you know. Thanks for the help, Inspector."

"Stay alert, Em and Em," Nathan replied.

"He's a good man," Zinger said when Wells was out of earshot.

"One of the best," Nathan agreed.

There was a moment of silence as the captain took a look around the empty room and lowered his voice.

"I spoke with LEOs in New Mexico," he started. "About your girl."

Nathan gave Zinger his full attention.

"They had security at the airport waiting for her. They weren't going to arrest her, but they *were* on the lookout." Zinger shook his head. "No one saw her come in."

Nathan relaxed. "Steve, you know that doesn't mean anything. Emily's a master escape artist."

"You're not hearing me." Zinger's eyes held Nathan's. "They did a full sweep, looking for Nancy's name rather than Emily's. No Nancy ever checked in to the flight."

Nathan let the captain's words sink in. She never checked in. Of *course* she didn't, he realized. That would put her in a bind. There would be a way to track her. He should have known she was too smart for that. So now...he had nothing. Emily could be anywhere. His chest rose and fell with his frustrated sigh. He looked off with a nod.

"Of course."

"Sorry, Detective. I've got my people on the lookout. Had to cash in a few favors."

"Keep me posted."

The doors opened as Shellie finally emerged from the lab. Her eyes locked on the men, a small smirk touching the corners of her mouth. "I know what it is."

⸎

"IT'S A LIFE FORM."

Nathan looked at the computer screen over Shellie's shoulder. "What *kind* of life form?"

She lifted a finger. "*That* I don't know."

"What do you mean you *don't know?*" Zinger pressed.

"Science has only come so far, boys."

She double clicked on a small photo of the blue substance, expanding it on the screen. The blue splotch rotated slowly under an italicized title.

"*Unknown species. Possible Ext.,*" Captain Zinger read. "Ext.?"

"Extraterrestrial," Shellie said.

"You can't be *serious*," Nathan said.

"That's what the computer came up with. It's a parasite. Once it finds a host, it invades and attaches to the brain. Then it looks for food. It understands that the body needs to be fed or it will die. It *doesn't* seem to understand what's okay to eat."

Nathan stared at the screen. "Come to think of it, every report was about this thing attacking someone."

Shellie nodded. "That makes sense. From what the computer was able to gather, the form feeds on live beings so it assumes the body does as well."

"Even though it's attached to the brain?" Zinger asked. "Wouldn't it learn what to eat there?"

"I think it only takes over the motor functions."

"How do we get rid of it?" Nathan asked.

"I'm surprised you were able to get me a sample at all," Shellie said.

"What do you mean?"

"Same as last time." She nodded toward the screen. "There was hardly enough of this little beauty to test."

He shook his head. "But I brought it straight from the scene. It couldn't have been longer than fifteen minutes." Nathan looked back at the screen. The blue substance hovered in the white field. "What are you..?"

"I call it the Rush."

Zinger's twisted his face. "The Rush?"

Shellie nodded proudly. "I named it myself."

Nathan scoffed. "You couldn't come up with anything better than Rush?"

"*The* Rush. I named it after its effects. When this little guy invades a body, the person goes through sensory overload. Bright sunlight, an intense sense of smell, extreme sensitivity to touch, etcetera. It overpowers the person, driving them insane. Then, you're at its mercy."

"Does it kill?"

Shellie's lips pressed to a thin line as she shook her head. "I don't know if it's the parasite itself that kills or the depression of nutrients in the body that eventually shuts it down. I wasn't able to bring Debbie back before she died."

"Debbie?"

"One of my little mice. There was just enough left from the raccoon to take over Debbie's body. She didn't even last five minutes, but that might be because she's small. In a human, it might take hours."

Nathan went for the door. "I have to talk to the Epsons."

"Wait...Nathan!"

"Just call me!"

Shellie sighed.

"He never was a patient one," Zinger said.

"There's more. Remember how we thought the stuff was deteriorating?" Zinger nodded. "It wasn't deteriorating like that. This is a very dependent life form. It needs to stay close to whatever birthed it or it will die."

Zinger scowled. "You mean...there's a *mother*?"

"Or a mad scientist." She pointed to the screen. "It needs to stay close to...wherever it came from. The further away it gets, the shorter its life span."

"Then it's coming from somewhere on Comfort Lane," Zinger surmised.

Shellie nodded as she looked at him over her shoulder. "There's one more thing. Once the host dies, it's very eager to find another. It turns itself into some sort of vapor so it can escape, otherwise it would die with the body." Her eyes became intense as she looked to the captain. "Anyone close to the vapor will be infected."

Zinger scowled at the news. "Nathan and Wells saw the vapor come out of the raccoon."

"If they were close enough to inhale it, one of them might be infected."

"Is there a cure?"

Shellie shook her head. "Not that I've found; there hasn't been a sample that's lasted long enough for me to test."

Zinger pulled out his phone, walking out of the lab. "You're invaluable, Shellie."

"Don't ever forget it."

———— ❧ ————

NATHAN KNOCKED ON THE EPSON'S FRONT DOOR, checking his watch as he waited for a reply. It was quite early in the morning; *he* certainly wouldn't have been awake if not for this. He waited a moment longer and knocked again more forcefully. No answer. Nathan pressed the doorbell several times, hearing it ringing through the door. Still nothing. He took a quick look around before trying the knob.

The door creaked open. He ignored the chill he felt and made his way into the dark home, quickly shutting the door behind him. From his waistband, he took out his small .40 Glock. Silence rang in his ears. The *tick-tock* of a clock added an extra element to the eerie interior. Dim light from outside glowed around the blinds in the living room. He jumped when his phone vibrated in his pocket. Without taking it out, he reached down and pressed a button through his jeans, silencing the phone.

Nathan made his way down the hallway. A familiar, foul odor hung in the air as he crossed the threshold. He could just see the door standing ajar at the end of the hall in the darkness. His phone vibrated again, and again he silenced it as he made his way down the hall.

When he pushed the door open, hundreds of tiny blue eyes turned and looked at him. A dark form lay in the bed, cast in the shadows of the dim room. What looked like hundreds of rats fed on the gnarled body.

"Shit!"

Nathan slammed the door and took off down the hall. He heard tiny bodies slamming against the door as he darted around the corner, then it splintered. The hairs on the back of his neck stood on end as he fumbled with the door knob to make his escape. His skin crawled with apprehension. He knew they were after him. He opened the door to freedom.

A silhouette stood in front of him, blocking his escape. Before he could react, a blow to his head sent pain down his spine. Darkness tunneled in as he fell to the ground. Police sirens were distant in the air. The last thing he saw was the silhouette reaching for him.

CAPTAIN ZINGER TURNED WHEN HE HEARD THE AUTO-matic doors open. Three officers entered, their faces forecasting bad news.

"Anything?" he asked before they reached him.

The officers shook their heads. "We can't even find his car," one said.

"Did you check his house?"

"We broke in. He wasn't there. You should see his room, Captain. He's obsessed with that Emily chick. It's all over his wall and on the computer scr—"

"I don't give a damn about what he does in his spare time." Zinger said. "Did you find him?"

Again the officer's shook their heads.

"Keep looking."

He folded his arms as he looked out the window, waiting. The night couldn't have been any worse. He thought they were finally going to get a break in this Comfort Lane case. Shellie's information gave them a big piece of the puzzle. With the strange things only happening on one street, they knew where to search. But now...now he didn't know what to think. Nathan's disappearance was unsettling. There wasn't a trace. Only one person had a reputation like that. He didn't like the implications.

"They still haven't found him?"

Sergeant Brad Nelson's faded reflection watched him in the window. He was a tall, lean man with sheep-like features. A good sergeant. Lord knew he needed one right now.

Zinger shook his head. "Not even a clue."

"At all? They didn't find his car or anything?"

"Nothing. Last place he said he was going was the Epson's, but we can't search the place with no evidence."

"Do we know he ever made it there?"

"No. We don't even know if he just skipped town. His car isn't at his house."

"Maybe he's at Sonya's."

Zinger shook his head. "He wouldn't do that now. Not after what he learned about The Rush."

"What's the Rush?"

"That's what Shellie calls this thing that's fucking up Comfort Lane."

Nelson hesitated. "Do you think maybe...Nathan was infected?"

"We would have found something."

In the glass, Zinger saw Nelson glance around the room before lowering his voice. "Do you think it's her?"

Zinger checked the man's resolve and found it rock solid. "I wish I could say no."

The sergeant sighed through his nose. "So what do we do now?"

"Can't do anything without evidence. I don't know where Nathan is, but for now he's on his own."

The automatic doors opened and a cold breeze rushed in. A man pushed a wheelchair in with a woman who was slouched over. The nurse at the front desk asked him to sign in and pointed him to the waiting area. The man eyed all of the officers in the waiting room as he wheeled the woman next to an empty chair and sat down. The telephone at the front desk rang as Zinger watched a group of officers head outside, probably for a smoke. The new "Tobacco Free" department policy didn't extend to those who were already smoking prior to its effective date.

Zinger sighed. What a god-damned mess. First Lydia, now this. A missing person and another victim. This thing on Comfort Lane was becoming more of a headache every week. Up till now they had managed to keep the media out of it, but he wondered how long that would last. Hell, all of the cameras on one street might work to their advantage.

His stomach growled and his eyelids were heavy. It had been over eighteen hours since the Captain had last slept. Sunlight was beginning to lighten up the sky; the orange and purples were fading into the darkness of the early morning. He needed a hot breakfast and a good cup of coffee. There was a Starbucks around the corner from the hospital. Maybe he could grab a quick bite.

"Excuse me, Captain Zinger."

He looked up to see the front desk nurse standing in front of him. He hadn't even seen her coming.

"Yes?"

"There's a phone call for you."

THE CAPTAIN LIFTED HIS CHEST TO THE FOB BOX NEXT to the door. The red light on the box flashed green as it beeped and the electronic latch clicked. The room behind was dark save for the tens of computer screens throughout. Dispatchers sat before groups of three, all of them speaking into headsets and typing on the keyboard. A hand waved him over from the far side of the room. Angela, one of their best, finished off a call as he rounded her desk. She rolled a strand of dirty blonde hair behind an ear with her meaty hand. Her hazel eyes remained locked on the screens.

"What's up?" Zinger asked.

"One of the cameras outside the department went out," she explained.

Zinger upturned a palm. "...So?"

Angela furiously typed on the keyboard, pulling up a recording of the camera. "When it came back on, *this* was on it."

A torn piece of note paper covered the camera's view. A message was scribbled sloppily in black. Zinger leaned over Angela's shoulder to get a closer look.

*If you want to find Nathan meet me at 5th and Vine.
Alone.*

"You are still looking for Nathan, right?" Angela asked.

"Can you print this out?"

She nodded. "You know where it is."

Zinger headed toward the door. "Thanks."

"Mmhm."

He grabbed the printout and looked over it again, not recognizing the writing as anyone he knew. 5th and Vine...one of the darkest parts of the city. Whoever it was didn't want to be seen. Zinger pulled out his phone. He needed officers.

BLOWN STREETLIGHTS CAST THE PARKING LOT BEHIND the Walgreens at 5th and Vine in darkness. Dark, secluded, abandoned...ominous. Fits the usual for a person who doesn't want to be seen. Zinger sighed as he parked the unmarked car down the street and climbed out. His heart pounded as he went to the lot, his eyes searching everything. Though he always had his firearm on him, he was completely exposed right now. Anyone looking to kill him would have it easy. He was getting too old for this shit.

Casually, he walked past the lot. No one was waiting there for him. Through the windows, the inside of Walgreens was cast in shadows.

"I wasn't sure you got my message."

Zinger froze at the honey perfect, sing-song voice. His looked to the right. Walgreen's outer wall looked back at him. She was in the shadows in the corner. He had walked right past her.

"Where's Nathan?" Zinger asked.

"Whether or not you rescue him depends on how well you follow directions."

Zinger quickly grew tired of the game. "What do you want, Emily?"

She was silent when a car drove by. "How far are you going to go to help Nathan?"

"Why do you care?"

She was silent, calculating.

"We're considering this a hostage situation," Zinger said.

"You should, because it is."

"Tell me where he is."

"The rush is on. Is the north warehouse still abandoned?"

As quietly and quickly as he could, he made his way around the corner. "That warehouse has been demolished for years. What does that matter?"

He darted around the corner when silence answered him. The shadows were empty. Zinger looked to the ground. No footprints. No smeared dust. Nothing. Absolutely nothing. It was like no one was ever there. He turned, scanning the parking lot. He was alone in the shadows.

As he walked back to his car, reds and blues came from either end of the road. Zinger sighed as officers parked in line with his vehicle and jumped out. They shouted at him as they approached. He lifted a hand to say he was alright.

"Did she say anything?" one of them asked.

"I need a radio."

NATHAN AWOKE TO THE SOUND OF CLINGING METAL. HE had to blink several times to clear up his blurry vision. A long metal lab table stood in front of him. The bright light beaming down on the table was so bright he couldn't see beyond it. A man in jeans and an Under Armor shirt hunched over the table with his back to Nathan. In the background a low rumbling noise could be heard between the ringing metal. The surrounding walls were a dull brown. He realized they were in a cave.

Nathan tried to move and realized his hands were tied behind his back and his feet to the chair. Another dull light stole his attention to the right. In the wall behind him, what looked like a fish tank had an illuminated blue liquid. The angle forbid Nathan from seeing what was inside the tank. Still...he thought he'd seen it before.

A pounding in his head made him wince and forced out a grunt of pain. The clanging stopped and the man looked over his shoulder. A white medical mask was over his nose and mouth. The man's thick brows lifted in mild interest.

"It's about time you woke up," the man said without facing him.

"Where am I?" Nathan demanded.

"That doesn't matter anymore. At least, it won't soon enough." The man put down the tool he had been using. "You know, I used to sit and ask myself why life was like this. Why things went wrong at the most inopportune times. Once again, life didn't disappoint." He looked at Nathan over his shoulder. "Why couldn't you just leave it alone? I was so close. So *close*."

"So close to what?" Nathan asked.

"To finding the cure."

"You mean for The Rush?"

The man shook his head. "No. The cure for what they say is incurable." He reached over the table and picked up something. "For what they *refuse* to cure." His voice broke. "For what my little girl was dying of."

"What little girl?"

Nathan knew. He knew who the man was as soon as he had heard the voice, but he needed to keep him talking. Strangely, the man's voice was different from before. Deeper. *Deeper*? No, more grated. Almost as if he had a sore throat.

"Don't play stupid," the man said. "You know who I'm talking about."

So much for that.

"Lydia died because of the Rush."

The man looked at Nathan. Not so much with curiosity but more interest, intrigue. Like a scientist observing an experiment. "That's the second time you've said that. What's the Rush?"

"The parasite that's been all over Comfort Lane. We've figured out what it is."

"A parasite?" The man chuckled. "You know nothing. It's not a parasite. It's a symbiotic organism. I developed it myself." He walked to the illuminated glass case. "The perfect organism. We provide the nutrients it needs to survive in this world, and in return it ensures that we do."

Now Nathan was intrigued. "What do you mean?"

"It heals us completely, whatever the circumstance. Do you understand? Any disease or sickness or injury would no longer be a problem. All you have to do is survive."

This man was crazy. He actually thought he had created a creature that healed everything? Why would anyone even *try* to do that? It's not like it mattered. Everyone was going to die anyway. Then Nathan remembered something he had said before.

"Your daughter was dying before the Rush got her," he said.

The man stared at the water. "This would have healed her. She would still be here and she wouldn't ever have to worry about anything again."

Nathan finally grasped the man's meaning. "You really think you found the cure to cancer, Mr. Epson?"

Mr. Epson whirled to him. "Not just cancer. *Everything*. I found the cure to weakness, fatigue, disease. Anything that causes the body to fail. I found immortality. Do you see now? The implications of what we could accomplish are just..."

"So what happened then? Why is Lydia gone?"

Mr. Epson swallowed and looked back to the tank. "I made a mistake. I mixed the wrong components together and one of the strands went unstable. Somehow the rat got out of its cage while we were sleeping and made it outside. The strand puts its DNA in its victims and they become infected."

"But if you have a pure strand, wouldn't that cure the infected?"

Mr. Epson's eyes came back to Nathan, impressed. "You understand. But then you have to catch them. It took a while; I had to read police reports to find them, but I caught them all. There were only a few scattered cases of outbreak, luckily, but that was how I learned about the spread. Anyone bitten didn't survive the next night. Then they became infected."

Nathan scowled. "Then you lied to me at the hospital."

Mr. Epson returned to the table and nodded. "I tried to get her away. I knew she didn't have much time, but my wife was so worried she never let Lydia out of her sight. She had no idea what I was working on." He flipped a hand. "She wouldn't have listened to me anyway."

"But Forensics didn't find anything foreign inside Lydia's body."

"Because it isn't a foreign creature. It adapts to the body, otherwise its defense system would try to destroy the symbiote."

It actually made sense. The computers were programmed to look for things that weren't consistent with the human body, but if a creature was able to adapt itself, it would be able to travel through the body with ease.

When the person died, it would be no different than any of the other thousands of bacteria in the body.

"Where's your wife now?" Nathan asked.

"Dead. Apparently more than one rat got out. Maybe one was infected by the other who infected another. I woke up next to them feeding on her."

"They killed her and not you?"

Mr. Epson turned to Nathan. Something in the man's eyes rose panic in Nathan's chest.

"They see me as their father," Mr. Epson explained. He walked back to the tank. "And they're right. I have to save them. I can't see any more of my creations die."

He pressed a button on the tank and Nathan heard a whir. Mr. Epson again returned to the table with a capsule in his hand. Nathan could see the illuminated liquid in it. The same color that he'd found in the dirt. The same color as the vapor that drifted out of the raccoon's mouth. The same color as whatever was all over Lydia. The pieces slammed together in Nathan's mind.

Mr. Epson lifted a syringe from the table and drew the liquid into it.

"It doesn't have to be like this, Mr. Epson," Nathan said.

He nodded. "Yes it does. I can't let you go free and I can't kill them. They're all I have left. You will be the one who saves them. *If* you survive."

"What?"

Mr. Epson dropped the now empty capsule and approached him. Nathan wrestled with the ropes that bound him. In his effort, he toppled his chair trying to free himself. He heard a sickening pop as the side of the chair slammed down on his arm. Pain exploded down to his fingers, forcing out a scream Nathan hoped would be heard by someone. Anyone.

Wherever they were.

Mr. Epson righted the chair. A pinch stung Nathan's neck as Mr. Epson injected the liquid into him.

"You'll be unconscious shortly," Mr. Epson said softly. "And if you wake up you'll be the key to stopping this madness. I hope you understand. Your sacrifice will save this entire town. Maybe even the world."

"What sacrifice?" Nathan managed.

Mr. Epson went back to the table to put down the syringe. "The unstable strain will have to feed on your body to get the cure. Once they get your blood into their systems, they will be restored. If you survive this, you won't survive that."

Nathan finally understood what the low rumble was. It wasn't something in the distance. It was The Rush from somewhere deeper in the cave. Mr. Epson walked out of eyesight behind the bright light.

"May the Lord have mercy on you."

Nathan was suddenly alone. The pain in his arm discouraged any movement. He then tried rubbing his chair leg against the dirt, hoping a rock would slice the ropes.

The rumbling closed in on him.

He could see the illuminated eyes round the corner and settle on him. Nathan rubbed faster as panic welled up in his chest. The air caught in his throat as they made for him. Tears of desperation welled.

Oh God!

Heat suddenly overpowered his body. Nathan broke out in a sweat as he began panting. The table was toppled by their numbers. Their eyes burned into him. The first to reach him took their bites, sending sharp stabs of pain through his body. He tried to flinch back, but the ropes held him still. Darkness funneled in. Angry eyes and teeth were the last thing he saw.

CAPTAIN ZINGER PERKED UP WHEN HIS LIEUTENANT came into the office. Nelson shook his head.

"They weren't there."

Zinger rose from his chair. "What..?"

"There were just a bunch of boxes. No one was there. There wasn't even a sign that someone had *been* there."

Zinger looked off. "Son of a bitch. She tricked us."

He shook his head as he walked to the window beside his desk. Had he misinterpreted her message? It didn't make sense. She asked about the warehouse. Clearly that's where she wanted him to go.

"Did she say anything else?" Nelson asked.

He had one way of getting into the Epson's house, but it was risky. Career-ending risky. If he was right, he just might save Nathan's life. If he was wrong...

"I want to look at the warehouse myself," Zinger said. "Take some men to the Epson house. Get in there and check it top to bottom. If there's a napkin out of place, I want it checked out."

"But we have no reason to—"

Zinger fixed the man with a glare. "I said get in there, Lieutenant."

Nelson snapped his mouth shut. "Yes sir."

Zinger settled back into his chair and let out a sigh. As he reached for his phone, it rang.

"Zinger."

"Hi, Captain, it's Joy."

He drew in a deep breath. "Hello Joy."

"I...I know you're not supposed to talk about it, but..." Her voice broke. *"Have you guys found anything yet?"*

He pressed his lips together. The poor girl.

"You know how it is, Joy. I can't talk about it."

He fought with his own emotions as he listened to her cry. Damned protocol. After a moment she finally controlled herself enough to speak.

"Okay. Will you call me if you find anything?"

"Joy—"

"No...I know you can't. Just...I'm sorry. Forget I called."

The line went dead. Zinger sighed again before hanging up the receiver.

"Damn it, Nathan," he said aloud to himself. "Where the fuck are you?"

His frustration was beginning to wear on him. He knew it was a lost cause. He needed to treat this like every other case. But, damn it, this wasn't just another case. Still, he had a job to do.

He picked up the phone again and pressed three numbers. The line rang twice before a voice answered.

"Chief, it's Zinger. We've got a situation...We might have to address the media."

CHAPTER FOUR

CAPTAIN ZINGER WATCHED AS THE CASKET WAS LOW-ered into the ground. Tens of people surrounded the grave, their expressions all somber in the murky after-noon. Just fitting, he thought. A rainy day for a funeral. Could Mother Nature be any more fucking cruel? He couldn't help but reprimand himself. He should have realized Wells was in danger. He should have told him to get checked out as soon as he learned the two of them had found the raccoon.

And it made him even more anxious about Nathan's condition. He should have been long dead by now. Why hadn't they found anything?

He sighed, taking a look around at the people gathered. Most were officers from the department. Wells' fiancé and little boy. Some old college friends. His eyes went to the casket again. A damn good lieutenant, he was. His best. Victim to a parasite they didn't know the cure for.

He drove back to the department in silence, his thoughts still on Nathan. He couldn't understand it.

There was something they had missed. Some clue they hadn't found. But the officers had searched that place top to bottom. *He* had gone over it several times. Not even the media had turned up anything. Strangely, though, after Nathan had gone missing, the reports about the Rush also disappeared. Comfort Lane was once again a normal street, and Zinger had placed more police presence there. He shook his head as he drove. It just didn't make any sense.

He'd had several missing persons cases where the people were never found and presumed dead. Children among them. Children he had seen one day and were missing the next. Those cases always left a mark, but this one was different. First Wells, and now Nathan. They weren't like the rest. They were friends.

A knock on his office door brought Zinger out of his thoughts. He realized he was staring at the folder of the Comfort Lane case. He looked up to see Lieutenant Nelson in the doorway.

"You busy?" Nelson asked.

Zinger frowned and shook his head. The lieutenant came in and sat in one of the chairs. They sat in silence for a moment.

"Nice funeral," Nelson finally said.

"Yeah," Zinger agreed.

Another silent moment.

"I didn't know Wells had a son," Nelson said.

Zinger nodded. "He's six, I think. Plays football."

"Like his dad."

"Yeah."

The rain dotting against the window could be heard over the cool air rushing through the vent.

"Well I, uh..." Nelson pointed behind him with a thumb. "I, I should probably..."

"Yeah." Zinger nodded. "Yeah."

He found himself alone once again. He opened a drawer and took his copy of Nathan's file from atop his desk. With the other, he found the chronological spot for it. The trail had gone cold; Nathan was presumed dead. He held the manila folder over the spot.

There was something off about this case. Nathan was too smart to just be captured and killed. Or maybe he wasn't. Nathan was just a man, like he was. Like they all were. He could have been surprised or ambushed.

So why couldn't he drop the file into the drawer? Was he admitting defeat if he did or, even worse, giving up?

He shut the drawer, putting the manila folder back on his desk and rose, grabbing his coat on the way out.

SHELLIE TYPED AWAY IN THE FORENSICS LAB, STILL DRESSED in her black clothes from the funeral. Letters and images flew on her screen. Zinger's steps echoed in the wide room as he approached. He was able to identify figures on the screen as he closed the distance. He smiled. It was nice to know he wasn't the only one.

Shellie shook her head. "I don't understand."

"That's something I never thought I'd hear you say."

"It doesn't make sense. It just *disappeared.*"

Zinger grunted. "I haven't even read a report about it since Nathan went missing."

"One week the Rush is everywhere, then it's gone." She snapped. "Just like that. It stinks."

"So, you haven't found anything either, huh?"

Shellie pressed a button that blackened the computer screens. "No," she said, letting out a frustrated breath. "Steve," she looked at him over her shoulder, "you don't really think he's dead, do you? I mean they never found a body..."

"You've seen what happens when someone is exposed to the Rush. Are you really surprised they never found him?"

She let his words sink in and shook her head. "No, I suppose not."

Zinger patted Shellie on the shoulder. "The case is cold, Shellie. We don't have anything here. We can't do this forever."

She breathed a laugh. "Don't give me that, Steve. You're not fooling anybody."

She called out to him as he was leaving.

"There is something that I always wondered about."

Zinger looked back at her.

"Why did she come back?"

His brow tightened. "Who?"

"Emily. What could she have possibly wanted? And why would she give you that clue without explaining it if she really wanted to save him?"

Zinger shook his head. It was the question he had replayed in his head over and over and over again. He had never figured out Emily's riddle about the warehouse.

"I don't know."

"Do you know where she is?" Shellie pressed.

Zinger lifted a brow at her.

"Of course not," Shellie said, nodding at her own stupid question.

"Shellie," Zinger continued to the doors. "If you come up with anything, let me know. And to answer your question, no."

"No what?"

Zinger stopped at the doors and looked back. "I don't think he's dead."

———— ⋘⋙ ————

Zinger was sifting through papers when his desk phone rang. His eyes went to the clock. Quarter to six. He could let it ring; it was probably Joy again.

"This is Zinger."

"Zinger. Chief Tipton."

He stiffened. "What can I do for you, Chief?"

"Why have you not shut down the search on the McLain case?"

"I've received information that he might still be alive."

"Information from who?"

"It's complicated."

Chief Tipton was silent a moment as Zinger's words sank in.

"I'll call you back."

The line went dead and Zinger's cell rang a moment later.

"Did she contact you directly?"

"Yes," Zinger admitted.

"Why didn't you arrest her?"

"I never saw her."

"What did she tell you?"

"She asked if the warehouse was still abandoned. That was it."

The Chief was silent again. Zinger could almost hear him thinking.

"Did you find anything?" Tipton asked.

"No sir."

"Any clues at all?"

"No, sir."

"Shut it down, Captain."

"Sir, she wouldn't have contacted me unless—"

"Then why the hell didn't she tell you where to find him?"

"I believe she did, sir. I just think we haven't looked hard enough."

"You've been looking long enough. You know how it goes, Steve. After forty-eight hours it's damn near hopeless without a lead. It's been four days. Do you have any leads?"

Zinger sighed. "No sir."

"Then we're not wasting any more resources on this. Shut it down, Captain."

"Yes sir."

The line went dead.

Zinger put the phone back in his pocket as he took a deep breath. As much as he hated to admit it, the Chief had a point. He had torn that warehouse apart looking for clues, doing everything but digging it up. And he'd found nothing. His heart was heavy as he picked up his desk phone. Stopping the search would declare Nathan lost.

He dialed the numbers to the officers on the scene.

⸎

THE COLD GROUND WELCOMED HIS CONSCIOUSNESS AS he slowly came awake. He blinked at his blurry vision, and when he was able to focus he came face to face with a dead rat. His body jolted backward and his back slammed against something hard, causing it to rub on the dirt floor. The ropes that tied him to his chair were chewed. He sat up. Surrounding him were animals, all dark and all dead.

He'd hoped it was all a bad dream.

Nathan dared to inspect one of them. They didn't look injured. It was like they'd just keeled over. What the hell happened to all of them?

His senses suddenly kicked in; the smell of mold, dirt, and decay flooded his nostrils. There was also a sweet smell he couldn't identify, and yet it was familiar to him. Chills suddenly rippled goose bumps throughout his body and he winced at the light still beaming down on the now spotless operating table. His phone, wallet, all of his possessions were in his pocket. Even his car keys. Mr. Epson hadn't taken anything.

At the thought of his captor, everything came back to him. Images of his ordeal flashed through his mind – his capture, waking in the cave, being injected with the Rush. Nathan's hand went to his neck. It was sore, and the skin was raised.

But he was alive. How was he alive?

The tank was void of light. Nathan shot up and went to have a closer look. It was drained clean. His mind reeled in alarm. If Mr. Epson believed he had found immortality, he might try to use the symbiote on others. But he could be anywhere by now. How was Nathan going to find him?

He realized he was panting and took a frantic look around. An opening in the wall across the room gave the hope of freedom. He stepped over the dead animals and made for it. Lights were evenly spaced in the ceiling, providing just enough brightness to see ahead. The cave seemed to go on forever, but he finally came up to a dead end. A ladder led up a dark hole. He snatched his hand back when he bumped into the ceiling as he reached for the next rung. He felt it give a little, and then he thought he heard something beyond. Mr. Epson could be up there, waiting for him. The man seemed to be one step ahead. It was like he knew Nathan was going to come back to the house that night when he was captured.

Nathan was unsure how deep the lab went, but he knew he didn't want to be underground anymore. Whatever waited for him above, he would face head on.

With a grunt of effort, he pushed at the ceiling.

A silhouette turned at the disturbance, beaming a light at his face.

"Nathan?!"

Nathan recognized the voice. "Steve."

Captain Zinger rushed to his side, helping him out of the hole. He laid Nathan down, and he was content to stay on the ground, finally feeling free. Zinger knelt over him, stammering.

"What...how did..."

"Would you get that light out of my face?" Nathan said.

Zinger flicked it off. "Where the hell have you been? We were...where *were* you?"

Nathan shook his head. "I...don't really know."

Zinger pulled out his cell phone and dialed a number. He screamed his location into it before helping Nathan to his feet. "Let's get you to a hospital."

"I don't need—"

"You look like hell, and you haven't been seen or heard from in a week. You need to get checked out."

Nathan's mouth dropped open. "A week...?"

———❦———

"YOU KNOW, YOU ALL DON'T HAVE TO *STARE* AT ME. I'M REAL."

Nathan looked around at the people who had come

to see him in the hospital. Word of his miraculous return had spread through the town quickly. Every day a new group of people came to visit him. Sonya was ever so generous. Nurse Joy had stopped by. Even the police chief had crawled out of his mountain of paperwork to give Nathan a visit. Now Shellie, Lieutenant Nelson, and Captain Zinger stood around the bed.

"I don't understand how so many officers missed a trap door," Shellie said, looking over at the two.

"It was buried in the ground," Zinger explained. "They would have had to dig up every inch of the warehouse to find it."

Shellie lifted a brow. "Still."

"So, there haven't been any reports of the Rush?" Nathan asked.

"Not since you disappeared. Everything's gone back to normal. The worst call we've had was an angry old man in a nursing home. He actually bit two of the nurses trying to clean him." Zinger shook his head. "I hope to God I don't get Alzheimer's."

For some reason, Nathan found that alarming. If he had been gone for a week, there were plenty of opportunities for Mr. Epson to use his creation. There was no telling how many people could be infected right now.

"Something on your mind, Nathan?" Zinger asked.

He nodded. "I'm wondering how he managed to get the both of us down that little hole."

"You think there's another way in?"

"There has to be. No way he got my unconscious body down that ladder by himself."

"Did you see another way out?" Shellie asked.

Nathan shook his head. "But I wasn't really looking that hard. I just wanted to get out of there."

"What'd you see down there?" Nelson boldly asked.

Nathan stared off, the ghosts of his capture resurfacing from the darkness of his mind. "He had it there. The Rush. It was in some sort of tank. He said that it was the answer to everything. The cure for any sickness or injury. Even cancer." He looked at the three of them. "He...injected me with it."

"What!" they shouted.

"I watched him do it. I was bound; I couldn't move or fight back or anything. All I could do was topple my chair." Nathan tested his arm and found it didn't hurt anymore. "I think I broke my arm trying to get away."

"Looks fine to me," Zinger said.

Shellie inspected it. "It's definitely not broken now."

Nathan nodded. "I know. I don't know how, but I'm still alive. After what he said, I wasn't expecting to be."

"I never thought I'd hear you say that, Nathan," Zinger said.

"I don't exactly *feel* like myself, either." Nathan rubbed his neck.

His phone buzzed on the end table.

"The doctor said you're dehydrated and a bit malnourished, but you're free to be released when you feel up to it," Shellie said.

An unknown number had sent him a text. Nathan sucked air through clenched teeth when he read it. Zinger was the first to respond.

"What is it?"

"It's a message," Nathan said. "It says, 'welcome to my world.'"

"Mr. Epson?"

"Has to be. He must have taken my number off of the phone. *Fuck!*"

"Do you have any idea where he could have gone?" Zinger pressed. "Did he say what he was going to do next?"

"He just said my sacrifice would save the town. What about his house?"

"We found his wife there," Nelson said. "She looked like her daughter."

Nathan knew that already. Where could the man have gone? He couldn't remember Mr. Epson saying anything that would give it away.

Wait...

Nathan snapped up. "I need a car."

Zinger tossed Nathan his keys. "Take mine."

"Where are you going?" Shellie asked. "He could be anywhere by now."

"No," Nathan said, rushing out the door. "He's still in town."

NATHAN SCOLDED HIMSELF AS HE SPED IN THE UNMARKED police cruiser. Traffic moved over when they saw him coming, for the most part. He should have seen it earlier. He should have known better than to rush out. He thought he had the cure for everything. And after Nathan had survived, he would have believed it worked. He couldn't have taken Nathan down the hole on his own. There had to be another way in. Someone like Mr. Epson would want to test out his creation on more than just Nathan. He would want the entire world to have what his daughter didn't.

Stupid, stupid, stupid!

His car jerked to a halt as he came up to his destination. The large brown warehouse loomed over him, its windows blown out and doors worn down. He took a moment to collect himself. After escaping, he had hoped he would never see this place again. And even worse, go back under.

He stepped through the ajar double doors and into the dark warehouse. The wind whooshed through the open windows, adding a chill to the darkness. Not the best atmosphere, especially for what he knew waited for him down below. He found the corner easily and gently pulled up the ground. The ladder led down into the darkness. Nathan took a breath and started down, pulling the trap door atop him.

The lab came quicker than he remembered and he cautiously stepped inside. The chair, his chair, was still upturned on the far side of the room. The table was there and the tank...

Several empty cages lined the right wall beside a wooden desk with papers scattered around it. Nathan picked up a paper. Mathematics and scientific theories. The bio-composition. He grasped the general concepts recorded. The symbiotes were a result of trial and error. Some of the experiments failed, causing the subject to go "unstable". The Rush, Nathan surmised. He picked up another paper. More of the subjects were tested with a different strand of the symbiotes. No positive results. Another report had one surviving rat. A marking on one of the papers atop the desk caught Nathan's attention. Circled in red at the bottom of the page was the number 97. The rest of the report showed the symbiotes had a ninety-seven percent chance of instability. Alarm rose in Nathan's chest. Was he really going to use the symbiotes with such a high percentage of failure?

He had used it on Nathan.

Nathan's heart pounded with anxiety. He needed to find Mr. Epson before it was too late. It could have already been too late. He had to be in a place where people were sick. Somewhere they wouldn't suspect him. Where he could blend in with everyone and still administer the symbiote. There were several places. He pulled out his phone.

Captain Zinger answered after one ring. *"Yeah?"*

"Are you still at the hospital?"

"Yeah."

"Get some officers to the emergency room and ICU. Tell the staff someone might be impersonating a doctor."

"You think he's here?!"

"Not for sure, but if he is he's going to try to use his symbiotes on anyone who's sick. He thinks it'll cure them."

"What?!"

"That's how The Rush started. If any of them bite a clean person, they'll be infe—"

Something Zinger said earlier flashed through his mind. And suddenly, he knew where Mr. Epson was.

— ⚬⚬⚬ —

"THE AREA'S SECURE, SIR."

Zinger nodded and the officer went off. The black uniforms and heavy semi-automatic weapons were armed and made ready. Nathan slid an extra magazine on his body armor. This was the very thing he was hoping to avoid when he left his old department. He had to go in, though. He was hoping that seeing Nathan alive would scare the man into making a mistake.

"There was no answer at the front desk," Zinger said, "which is unusual. Normally these people are quick to call us if an old guy farts. We haven't had any other violent reports in town."

Nathan set his jaw. It was just as he suspected. He looked over his shoulder at the entrance to the New Manor Nursing Home. A facility for the terminally ill – people on the way out. The perfect place to test the symbiotes. And there was no telling what the Rush would do to them. If the reports he read were accurate...

It was dark inside and dead silent. The sun was beginning to fall in the sky, casting more shadows than he had hoped on the building. One thing he knew about the

90

Rush: they were practically shadows in the dark. He took several deep breaths, attempting to calm his pounding heart. He readied his weapon and nodded to the Captain.

"What do you suggest?" Nathan said. "There are four floors and the Rush could be on all of them."

Zinger's face set in a dark scowl. "We take it one floor at a time."

⸎

THEY FILED IN SILENTLY. NATHAN TOOK THE HEAD. THE hallways were dark and empty, not at all normal for a nursing home. Especially just after the dinner hour. The cold air sent goose bumps up his arms. They went quickly, stealthily, stopping to clear all doors – opened or closed. The first floor seemed to take forever to clear, but it was empty. They stopped in the main lobby to regroup. A map of the facility showed two ways up to the second floor – an elevator and the stairs. Elevators were always a no-go.

A small force stayed behind as the second floor was cleared. The force moved up before the team advanced to the third. A group of people were seen in night gowns and plain clothes as they stepped into the common hall from the stairs. Their blue eyes illuminated in the darkness as the Rush noticed them. They darted down the hallway with impossible speed. Nathan knelt as he called them out and the force opened fire. They were faster than he remembered.

"What the fuck *are* those things?" one of his team asked.

"The reason we're here," Nathan whispered.

They encountered a couple more stray groups and took them down swiftly. The third floor was eventually cleared; only one floor left.

"The fourth floor has a service entrance on the roof," Zinger said as they looked over the map. "There's an elevator and a stairwell, like all the rest."

Nathan actually entertained the idea of using the elevator, to have some kind of surprise on their side. Mr. Epson had definitely hunkered down by now. He might even be expecting them to come up the stairs. As far as Nathan knew, Mr. Epson wasn't an expert on police procedure. Maybe the basics would surprise him enough. But he wasn't up there alone. There was no telling how many people were infected. Total capacity was just under two thousand. They didn't have enough firepower for that many of the Rush.

This had to end. If any one of those people got loose, the entire town would be like a scene out of The Walking Dead. The infection might not stop there. And to think he had watched that show and laughed.

"We take the stairs," Nathan said, reloading his weapon. "Just like always. I have an idea."

Zinger nodded. "Let's get this done then. Move out!"

HUNDREDS OF BLUE EYES TURNED TO THEM AS THE DOOR burst open. Triggers were squeezed; bullets went flying down the hall. The high pitched screams of the Rush caused Nathan to wince. A few of his team stopped shooting to cover their ears. A deadly move. Nathan tried to keep the Rush off of them, to give them time to recover, but they were too fast. He kept his focus on his lines, clearing out as many as he could. They were actually gaining ground on the hallway, cutting down more of the Rush than expected. Bullets were flying through those close enough and killing ones behind. Nathan knew it was inevitable, though, as he quickly reloaded his weapon. They would be out of bullets, and the Rush were still coming, even if they were being swiftly cut down. The noises were deafening. Nathan's arms were getting tired.

They had called up all of the backups left below for the final push. In order for the attack to work, they had to hold the hallway. It was wide enough to allow about nine men in shoulder to shoulder. They set up a wall with nine kneeling and nine standing. When one ran out of ammo, they shouted as much and another swiftly took their place. They even began advancing. The strategy saved them the most bullets and kept the friendly fire down. It was a spur of the moment theory.

And it was actually working.

The team was able to push forward to the lobby, keeping the Rush off of them for the most part. They suffered small casualties from the stray that managed to get through the onslaught. Nathan made sure to cut down any who had been bitten. The last thing they needed was one of their own to rise up and join the other side.

Just as they pushed past the lobby, one of the Rush dove forward. The old man was taken out in the air, but his momentum bowled him into six officers, punching a hole in their wall. Like a collective intelligence, the Rush made for the hole. Those who were still in position took out as many as they could, but the push proved to be too much. Nathan's heart leapt to his throat as the Rush tore into the S.W.A.T team.

"Get back!"

He made his way back to the stairs. The men who survived followed his lead. They tried to limit the ways that the Rush could come at them. The narrow stairs made their numbers count for nothing, until the Rush began jumping down atop them. The S.W.A.T. team was whittled down. There were more of the Rush than the weapons could keep up with. The cries of death soon became that of just men. Nathan backed his way into the second stairwell, Zinger and one other officer with him.

"What now?" Zinger asked, reloading his weapon.

Nathan took a moment to settle his breathing. He didn't know what to do now. They had to stop this here, but they were three men. What chance did they have now?

"Detective."

It was Mr. Epson's voice, more alien than before. Rage burned Nathan within. They retreated even more when they heard the Rush coming down the hallways, gunning down the faster ones. They took up positions on either side of the second floor stairwell.

"I know what you're doing, Nathan," Mr. Epson shouted from above. "You think you can pick us off little by little. You know better. You're different now."

Us?

"What does he mean by 'you're different now'?" Zinger asked.

Nathan shook his head. "He's insane."

The elevator dinged beside them. The Rush were coming down. Zinger cursed as they fled down to the first floor, hoping that the Rush hadn't beaten them there. If they did, it would all be over. They cleared the door ready to fire. It was all bare.

"It doesn't have to be this way, Nathan. All you have to do is surrender yourself, and no one else is hurt."

Zinger scoffed. "That'll be the day."

The three of them backed down the hallway toward the entrance. None of the Rush emerged. Nathan knew they didn't have much longer. They were either going to stop the Rush, or die trying. The way things were looking, it was leaning more toward the second. He had a decision to make. He understood what Mr. Epson said. He *was* much more than his job title now. He was the only one who could end this.

Nathan looked at the two members left on his team. Zinger glared at him.

"No, Nathan. You're not going in there."

"If you two don't get out of here, you'll be killed."

"So will you!"

Nathan shook his head. "I'm much more valuable to him alive. I have to do this on my own. It's the only way we can stop this."

"And if you lose? You expect me to just let this town become infected?"

"You already have the perimeter. If anything besides me comes out, you cook it." Nathan looked back down the hallway. "If I don't come out in an hour, make sure nothing survives this building."

Captain Zinger gave Nathan a grim look. "We thought you were dead once already. I didn't think that would be a premonition."

"This has to stop here, Steve. One way or another, this can't go on. You know what will happen if it does."

Zinger looked back down the hall again. He breathed a sigh. "I've seen a lot of shit in my life. I never thought I'd be here." He looked to his fellow officer. "Let's go."

The two of them sprinted down the hall. Zinger turned and looked Nathan in the eye.

"You have fifteen minutes."

"Understood."

Zinger's lips pressed into a thin line. The two of them shared a look, both knowing this might be the last time they saw each other.

"Good luck," Zinger finally said.

Nathan swallowed. "If I don't come out, tell Joy—"

Zinger was already shaking his head. "Tell her yourself."

Nathan walked to the entrance and locked the doors behind the officers. He turned to the hallway and reloaded his gun before walking down the hall.

"Mr. Epson, I give up."

Silence.

"You hear me? There's no one else in here. I'm all alone."

The elevator in front of him dinged. The doors opened and blue eyes stared out at him. He dropped his weapon and went to his knees with his hands on his head.

"I surrender."

EPILOGUE

⚭

THE RUSH ESCORTED HIM BACK UP TO THE FOURTH floor. The blue eyes that had rushed at him moments earlier made no advance as he walked past. They hungrily watched him, daring him to make a wrong move. As they cleared the stairs, the Rush filed in behind him, discouraging any escape. He watched them cautiously, not entirely sure that they weren't going to move in on him. The manor had been turned into a dark land of horrors.

"Don't worry," came Mr. Epson's voice. "They won't hurt you. I've given them strict orders not to."

His voice was even deeper than before. If Nathan was right, there was not much time.

He came into view on the fourth floor lobby. He was still a big man, if that's what he could be called. The darkness had begun to take over his body. Dark lines swirled in on his face, giving him a sinister look. His eyes glowed blue, but he was not like the monsters around him. He was self-aware, speaking to him with intellect.

It was a terrifying sight.

A smile crawled onto his face. "You survived. Tell me, how do you feel?"

Nathan stopped before the creature that used to be Mr. Epson. "Pissed off."

"I dare ask why."

"You know damn well why. You've been toying with people's lives. Look around you. These are all victims of your experiments. This is what happens when you think you know what is better for someone than they do."

"On the contrary. All of these people gave me consent. Those who were aware enough to speak at least. I left the ones who weren't alone."

So that explained the bodies they'd found.

"They had Alzheimer's, asshole!" Nathan said.

"Why are you getting so upset, Nathan? You were given the symbiote and survived. Do you understand what that means? It works. You can't get sick from anything. You will never have any type of cancer, your body will heal faster. Don't you remember your arm?"

Nathan's hand reflexively went to his arm. It had completely healed, and he was sure he had broken it.

"I didn't ask for this," Nathan said.

"I was trying to rectify my mistake, but this…this is better. You are the one who can cure us all."

"That's not true. I read the reports. The symbiote has a ninety-seven percent chance of failure. Even if you all drank my blood, there is a slim chance you'll survive."

Mr. Epson's smile remained. "You understood my reports?"

"I'm surprised someone as smart as you could be so stupid as to think you'd have any success here."

Finally, the creature's smile faltered a bit. "What are you talking about?"

"It doesn't take a scientist to understand why the body rejected the symbiote. Older bodies are less adaptable than younger ones. They don't heal as fast and they don't adjust to foreign substances being introduced into the body. Your ninety-seven percent was only based on the youngest of your rats."

Mr. Epson looked off. "Then my daughter would have survived."

His eyes lost some of their brightness and sadness dropped his expression. "If my wife would have just let me be alone, I would have given her the symbiote and she would still be here."

"There's no guarantee she would have survived," Nathan said. He lifted a hand, indicating to the darkness around him. "But she would have had a better chance than any of these people."

"And yet," Mr. Epson's eyes returned to Nathan, "here you are."

Mr. Epson rose from his throne of the Rush, who took their place behind him. He began slowly circling Nathan, who kept the man in front of him. "You really are special, aren't you Nathan McLain? Such a slim margin for survival, and here you are. I've tried literally hundreds of people here and none of them survived. Not one. Besides me, of course." He extended an upturned palm. "We are the narrow three percent."

"Actually that's not true, either. I survived with my mind intact. Yours is being slowly eaten away by the Rush."

Rage flashed in his eyes. "Stop calling it that! They are the symbiotes."

"*I* have a symbiote. *You* have a parasite. The darkness is spreading through your mind like a virus. Soon, you will be like them."

Mr. Epson studied Nathan like a father who had just witnessed intelligence in his offspring. "Yes. Soon I will be like them. I tried my symbiotes on these people and failed. I see now that their bodies and minds were too old to adapt. I'm not as old; my body adapted, but my mind is being consumed by the symbiote. But," his smile returned, "while they just feed to keep the body alive, I know how special you are, what your blood can do for my body. It can give my mind the awareness it needs to survive."

So that was his plan.

Nathan pulled out his pocket knife. "My blood will be staying inside me. Thanks."

Mr. Epson pointed. "But you're already bleeding."

Nathan looked down at his side. Three slashes sliced across the unprotected part of his body armor. Dark red bled through the black. He winced as pain suddenly slammed into him, dropping him to a knee. He managed to look up to see Mr. Epson casually approaching.

"You aren't in any condition to fight, not against all of us."

Nathan readied his knife. With Mr. Epson being infected, he would have to be fast. He wouldn't get many chances to strike.

When Mr. Epson was close enough, Nathan lunged. The blade caught air as Mr. Epson dodged the attack. Nathan rolled and whirled to face him again. Mr. Epson kicked at him and Nathan leaned back to dodge it. They faced each other again, the time for talking finished. Nathan brought his knife up. The Rush growled around him, but remained at bay. The two men circled the room until one ran at the other. They danced around the lobby, one attacking, the other dodging and counter attacking. A few blows were exchanged, and Nathan slashed Mr. Epson's arm one good time. The blue eyes around them watched, growling angrily as the fight wore on.

A kick to his chest sent Nathan to the ground. He lifted his head to see Mr. Epson running at him. He was going toward Nathan's good side, trying to force him to lean on his injury. Nathan jumped up and ducked under the punch, burying his knife into Mr. Epson's leg. He roared in pain and gave Nathan a powerful kick. The blow sent him airborne again, slamming him into the Rush along the wall. Blue eyes burned into him, teeth snapping at his face. Nathan slashed his knife through several of them. He was lifted from the ground and heaved toward the opposite wall. The wind was driven from his lungs as he crashed into it and fell to the ground. His vision became a blur. Again he was picked up. Mr. Epson held his shirt with one hand and brought his face close. He sneered before punching Nathan in the stomach. Reflexively Nathan tried to double over, but Mr. Epson held him up. It did nothing to ease the pain. Somehow he managed to hold his knife and he stabbed at Mr. Epson's heart.

A hand caught Nathan's wrist inches from his chest.

"You are a constant surprise, Nathan," Mr. Epson said. "You defeat the odds at every turn. Even now, with your body beaten and being outnumbered you still find the drive to fight."

Mr. Epson gave a twist that snapped Nathan's wrist. He screamed as the knife finally fell from his hand. Again he was tossed to the other side of the lobby. Pain shot through his body when he hit the hard, cold ground and slid into the wall. He winced, grabbing his broken wrist with his good hand in an attempt to ease the pain. Mr. Epson's heavy steps approached again.

"Once my mind has been healed, I will be able to use my blood to make more of the symbiote. I will be able to cleanse the world from what they said was incurable." He lifted Nathan up again. "I will be the savior of this species."

He took a hold of Nathan's stomach and twisted, pulling at his skin. Nathan's vision went white with pain. A deafening noise filled his ears until it was all he heard.

He wasn't in the room anymore. There were no more of the Rush. No Mr. Epson. No fighting. The deafening noise faded into the background until he could barely hear it. There was just her. She was laying against his chest as they looked out over the water. Like they always did. Her brown hair was let down, swaying slightly in the cool bay breeze. She sighed against him and looked up. Her cheeks, specked with dark freckles, fluffed as she smiled. He lifted a hand to her warm cheek and guided her lips to his. Her tongue touched against his before further exploring his mouth. When he parted, her eyes held a spark of maddening lust. They found his and she gazed up at him, her chest heaving as she panted lightly. Her tongue flicked out to lick her lips and she leaned in to his ear.

"It's mine now," she whispered.

His brow tightened as he turned toward her. Her hand plunged into his side.

The room came back to him. He realized the deafening sound from before was his own scream. Mr. Epson still held him off the ground. His smile welcomed Nathan back to the darkness, blood dripping from the corner of his mouth. Nathan looked down to see a hole in the unprotected part of his armor. Blood now dripped down over the dark fabric. His side burned as if he were being held over a fire. He could hardly keep his eyes open against the pain.

"Your sacrifice is appreciated," Mr. Epson growled.

Nathan was lifted higher, then the air rushed past him. A blow to his back and head added another element to the pain and a shattering chime followed. The window to the lobby came into his vision, jagged edges of glass revealing Nathan's fate. Glass shards floated in his vision as he drifted out of the hole in the window and began the long journey down. The Rush began filing around Mr. Epson as he watched Nathan fly out. The window drifted up in Nathan's vision and he saw the break between the third and fourth floor rise up, as if the building was lifting into the air.

The world suddenly went silent. It was almost peaceful, the air rushing at him. Were it not for the building, it would have been comforting. He closed his eyes, accepting the inevitable. It wouldn't be long now.

A crashing sound burst through the silence. Fire exploded out of the windows at the base of the building. The explosions traveled up, knocking out debris floor by floor. As he passed the second floor, the explosion shoved into his back, sending him flying outward. The air rocked with a final explosion as trees and grass rushed at him.

—◦◦◦—

"If not for these brave men, our city would have been infected with one of the worst viruses known to man. Therefore, on behalf of the City of Tenaple, I, Mayor Jones, award these heroes with the key to the city."

The crowd went wild before the podium. Captain Zinger sighed. What the hell was he supposed to do with a key to the city? It's not like the city was protected by gates that he could lock up at night. Besides, they had lost much more in that old manor than he had gained by surviving it. Mayor Jones, standing a head shorter than he with a receding hairline graying at the sides, pinned a medal on Zinger's chest and handed him a key. They shook hands.

"You've saved us all, Captain," the mayor said. "Nice work."

Zinger shook his head. "Just doing what you hired me for, sir."

The Mayor moved on to the Corporal, who had also been in the building.

It had been nearly a month since the incident at the old manor. The minutes had passed agonizingly slow for Captain Zinger, but Nathan never came out. The blast had crumbled the building, and the Rush was eradicated from the town. If nothing else, Nathan had managed to keep the parasite from spreading to the rest of the world. There was no telling how far the disease would have spread. It could have been the next plague. He took a deep breath. It was a sacrifice he would make sure no one forgot.

They went through the rubble, but never found Nathan's body. A city-wide search had turned up nothing. They found his car in the Epson's garage, but no body. Again. It was a moment of deja vu for the Captain, but he knew this time it was different. Blood was everywhere on the skeleton of the building. Forensic tests showed a substantial amount of it had been Nathan's. With the explosions, though, it wasn't unusual to not find a body. Perhaps he was too close to an oxygen tank or something. Maybe he lured the Rush in when the bombs went off. No one survived the blast, but the bodies were all free from the parasite. Even Mr. Epson's.

Now, the city was safe and back to normal with calls for runaways and assaults being the only excitement. Every now and again there would be a high-stress call, but nothing compared to the Rush. After all of this, he had a new definition of "high-stress". Even calls involving guns.

They had found the lab, eventually. The papers there were reviewed and burned by the Captain himself. He didn't understand most of it, but the ninety-seven percent failure rating stood out to him. It was alarming that a man would be desperate enough to chance using a parasite that had such a high rate of failure. He wondered what the man's drive was. Not that it mattered, now.

As he drove back to the police station, his thoughts settled on Nathan again. He wondered if there was a scant chance Nathan had made it out somehow. Knowing Nathan, it wasn't unlikely. He had survived the Rush.

Zinger still didn't understand that one, and he hadn't found the answer in the reports. Except that Nathan was part of that three percent. Three percent. Such a small margin of success and Nathan had found it. As he often did. He found Nancy's killer, after all. It was the same detective working the Emily Henderson case.

Emily Henderson.

Nathan would never find her, now. The reason for Nancy's death was all for nothing. Why would Emily need to find cover to get away from Tenaple? She was like an assassin – if she wanted to disappear, there wasn't a damned thing you could do about it. Why would she need someone to take on her identity?

At his office he took off his uniform and hung it on one of the hooks behind the door. His glossy desk still held the Epson case atop it. He plopped in the chair and pulled out the drawer, finding the proper place for it among those solved. While he looked, his eyes went to Nathan's file, sitting atop those unsolved. He had never actually filed it. He picked it up and stared at it for a while, then an idea came to him.

He searched the solved cases for Nancy Cummings'. He had to know why Emily had targeted Nancy. It was the least he could do. The city's best brain was gone, so the task fell to him. He was a police Captain, for God's sake. He had a lot of pull. There had to be something he could find out. Nathan was more than the best private investigator in Tenaple. He was a friend. He had helped the Captain keep his desk, even upgrade it a few times with the cases he had solved. He had to solve the mystery behind Nancy's death. It was the least he could do.

For him.

HIS EYES CAME OPEN AT THE SOUND OF VOICES. DOU-bled vision turned his stomach. He groaned at the ache in his body and tried to move.

"Oh my god, Doctor," a male voice said. "He's waking up."

"Impossible," came another male voice. "He couldn't have healed already."

Two heads came into his vision, one a bald white man with thin glasses, the other considerably younger. Probably an assistant.

"Nathan?" the older man said.

"Where am I?"

A light was beamed into his eyes. Nathan turned away from it.

"His vitals are stable," the assistant said.

"Unbelievable..." the bald man replied.

Nathan became more aware of his surroundings. The room around him was dark, save for the surgical light over him. He realized he was on an operating table, one that looked frighteningly familiar to the one back in the cave. Panic welled in his chest at being captured again. He tried to move and found his body was bound to the table.

"Let me go!" he said.

The assistant looked to the doctor, who nodded. A button was pressed and Nathan's bounds released him. He jumped off the table and retreated away from the men. They both had white lab coats on. The doctor lifted his hands.

"Just take it easy, Nathan."

"Who are you?" Nathan demanded. "Where the *fuck* am I?"

"I'll tell you everything. I just need you to calm down. Your vitals are still a little shaky."

"Back. Up."

The doctor stopped and took a couple steps back.

"Turn on the lights."

He looked over at his assistant and nodded. The assistant pointed.

"The switch is over there."

"Nice and slow," Nathan said.

He blinked at the bright light. The medical lab around him came to full life. There were no cabinets. The walls were bright and bare and the operating table was long. Too long, he thought. There were windows and a glass door behind the assistant.

"We aren't going to hurt you," the doctor pressed.

"Where am I?"

"You're safe."

"Where?"

"What's the last thing you remember?"

Against his better judgment, Nathan thought back. Memories of Tenaple flooded his mind. He remembered waking up in the hospital, going back to the underground lab. The manor...the Rush. Fighting with Mr. Epson.

And losing.

His head began pounding, pain took him to his knees. The images played back in his head. Mr. Epson had ripped out a piece of his skin and threw him out the window. The building was exploding... and he fell. He *fell*.

Oh God.

He looked up to see the doctor and assistant looking down at him. He was lying on the ground.

"Am I...dead?"

The doctor smiled and shook his head. "No. You're

very much alive." He helped Nathan sit up. "Do you recognize me?"

Nathan looked at the man again. Somehow, he did look familiar. The doctor smiled.

"We first met when Lydia was brought to the hospital."

Nathan's jaw dropped. "Dr. Stein?"

He nodded. "Good to see your memories are still intact. I wasn't sure if you'd survive. Your body was crushed when she brought you here."

"Who?"

Dr. Stein looked off, considering. "I suppose I have all the proof I need. Before I tell you, there's something you need to know. Everyone here is alike. All of us."

At first Nathan didn't know what the doctor was talking about. But something in Dr. Stein's eyes connected the dots.

"You have the symbiote?"

Dr. Stein nodded. Nathan looked at the assistant.

"Him, too," Stein confirmed.

The assistant spoke. "My name is Charles Olsen. I'm Dr. Stein's intern."

"Everyone you see here, in this place, survived. We're all the narrow three percent."

"But how?" Nathan asked.

Dr. Stein and Charles shared a look. "That's a more complicated story."

Nathan understood that. His story wasn't exactly quick or easily explained. He still didn't know how he survived at all. Twice, now.

"Are there only three of us?" Nathan asked.

"No," Dr. Stein replied. "You're the twelfth."

"Where are the others?"

"You'll see, soon. First things first. Things are different now. We aren't the same as we were before. You were brought here so that you could take your place among us. She's found all of us and brought us together."

Nathan's heart pounded. "Who?"

"She has many names, but you know her as Emily Henderson."

About J.K. Miller II

J. K. Miller II's future brother-in-law is in a rock band named Set It Off. They are "legit": signed and touring all over the world. (#inlawloveforSIO). He enjoys a multitude of music. His favorite artists are Usher, Michael Jackson, Justin Timberlake, and Jason Mraz. He loves huskies. His first was actually named after a wolf in his books.

*"Either enjoy the story
or write the story everyone enjoys."*
– J. K.

www.ingramcontent.com/pod-product-compliance
Lightning Source LLC
Chambersburg PA
CBHW071626140626
46555CB00021B/745